FOOD FIGHT

a guide to eating disorders for preteens and their parents

JANET BODE

Simon & Schuster Books for Young Readers

To Arlene Weber Morales
and Donna Chumas

SIMON & SCHUSTER BOOKS FOR YOUNG READERS

An imprint of Simon & Schuster Children's Publishing Division

1230 Avenue of the Americas, New York, New York 10020

Copyright © 1997 by Janet Bode

All rights reserved including the right of reproduction
in whole or in part in any form.

SIMON & SCHUSTER BOOKS FOR YOUNG READERS
is a trademark of Simon & Schuster.

Book design by Ethan Trask

The text for this book is set in 12-point Garth Graphic

Printed and bound in the United States of America

First Edition

10 9 8 7 6 5 4

Library of Congress Cataloging-in-Publication Data

Bode, Janet.

Food fight : a guide to eating disorders for preteens
and their parents / by Janet Bode.

p. cm.

Includes bibliographical references,
and comprehensive resource guide

Summary: A comprehensive guide to eating disorders,
discussing their causes, symptoms, and solutions.

ISBN 0-689-80272-2

1. Eating disorders in children—Juvenile literature.
[1. Eating disorders.] I. Title.

RJ506.E18B63 1997 96-29186

618.92'8526—dc20

contents

PART
I

For Young Readers

chapter 1

heavy meanings

Defining Moments

Eating disorders are mind-body problems. They occur when individuals reduce complicated lives to one issue: reducing their weight.

People may try to starve themselves, a condition called anorexia nervosa. They may binge and purge, uncontrollably overeating and then ridding their bodies of the food, a condition called bulimia nervosa. Or they may combine these two methods to lose weight, going back and forth between them.

Until recently most of those who developed anorexia and bulimia were in their teens or early twenties. Now the age when the behavior first starts can be even younger. Your age.

Although boys have been known to have eating disorders,

experts say that 85 percent to 90 percent of those they see are female. That's why this book is aimed more at girls than boys. That's why the words "she" and "her" will appear more often than "he" and "him."

Regardless of the gender, each person with an eating disorder is unique. Still they share certain characteristics. As they become increasingly focused on food and eating, their behavior falls into certain patterns. . . .

chapter 2

do you think
i'm too fat?

Poof!—I'm a Whale

Danielle, age ten: I was always asking my friends, "Do you think I'm too fat?" Everyone said no, but I thought they were lying. Anyway, I didn't feel happy about myself.

See, I was scared of being fat, that one day I'd wake up and—poof!—I was a whale. My thighs weren't that fat, but I just hated my waist. It was so wide. I felt awkward around my friends. While everyone else was a size 3/4 to 5/6, I was a 9/10. Wide waists run in the family on both my mom's and dad's sides.

My mom told me that when she was young, she had to learn by herself that she was fat and had to diet. Her mom never said anything about weight, and she thought she should have. So she started to encourage me to diet and exercise. She even said she'd buy me a workout tape.

We also had an exercise machine that I used three

times a week. But trying to make my waist smaller by working out—forget it. It was too difficult.

Now I'm on a serious diet. At first I only had three pieces of dry toast and five Cokes a day. But the more I lost, the less I ate. Then I figured, if I didn't drink anything, I'd lose even more. I just let myself have one small glass—five ounces—of water.

I am getting thinner. I'm down to size 1. But in my eyes that is not enough. It's never enough. Now my friends are telling me that I look horrible. My mom is freaking. She keeps saying "Eat" over and over. They don't understand.

I can't concentrate on anything. I cry all the time. Still, all I ever think about is food and how fat I am. I hate food! I promised my mom that if she won't make me go to the hospital for treatment, I'll go to group eating disorder meetings. I pray I'll get better, but I just don't know.

chapter 3

eaten
alive

Food Crazy

Anorexia.

It starts with a diet, a way to lose weight.

The person drops a few pounds, and the praise begins. "Wow, you sure look good," she hears from her parents.

"You've lost so much weight," she hears from her friends.

She takes that as encouragement to continue. She never considers that those words will lead her on a scary, unpredictable journey.

She doesn't know she will be the one who becomes obsessed with her diet. She will start to play mind games with herself as a misguided kind of logic develops. If losing five pounds is good, losing ten pounds is better. And losing fifteen pounds is better yet. One thing follows the other.

She invents different and strange ways of eating and living. Her only worry is food. She becomes food crazy. Her life revolves around the bathroom scale, a tape measure, and her calorie intake chart. Her body becomes her career and she is a true workaholic.

At first she cuts back to, say, 1,200 calories' worth of food a day—already a low figure. Then she tells herself, "That's not enough. Tomorrow I'll only eat 800 calories. And maybe by next week I'll go down to 400."

The Apple Ritual

The weight is coming off, but it is never enough in this girl's opinion. She sits alone on her bed grabbing and kneading an imaginary roll of fat on her belly. "Disgusting," she thinks, as she decides on refinements to her plan of attack.

If she eats a forty-calorie slice of apple, she'll round it up to an even hundred. If she has a single spoonful of cottage cheese, she'll add half the calories in the container to her count for the day. She never wants to undercount, and she'd always rather eat too little than too much.

By now she has decided that all food is evil. If she eats a whole peanut-butter-and-jelly sandwich, she's sure tomorrow she'll wake up weighing three hundred pounds.

STARVING FOR ATTENTION

Children between the ages of seven and ten, of average height and weight eat about 2,000 calories a day. Average girls from eleven to fourteen eat about 2,200 calories a day. Average boys that age eat about 2,500 calories a day.

Half that amount—1,000 to 1,250 calories—would be a semistarvation diet.[1]

She invents another trick, another ritual. She slowly cuts up the food into a gazillion pieces. It can take her an hour to eat next to nothing. Meals go into napkins to be hidden and later thrown away. At times she feels her throat freeze. Nothing will go down. Meat in particular seems hard to swallow.

She comes up with excuses for not having meals with her family. She starts turning down friends' invitations that might involve eating. That means no mall on the weekends, no pizza after school, no parties, no scout camp-outs, no beach picnics, no sleep-overs, no birthday celebrations, no real kid-shared hangout life at all. From Thanksgiving through New Year's, she's an emotional wreck.

Walking, Talking Encyclopedia of Food

In the beginning her parents and friends aren't aware of the dangerous power struggle she has entered. They have little idea they'll be swept up in her craziness. They often don't even notice what's happening.

Day by day, week by week, this girl is turning into a jumble of contradictions. She is a master of deception. She has a battle plan, and it's her secret. She diets and fasts and totals her calories and becomes increasingly skinny. But then she hides her thin body under layers of baggy clothes.

Suddenly they notice.

Those who love and care about her are stunned. This sweet daughter, this dear friend, has chosen to starve herself—possibly to death—in front of their eyes. They become frantic, horrified, angry, frustrated, and confused. How would you feel if someone special to you decided to stop eating? What would you do to try to stop her?

Often there are tears and bitter fights. "Eat your dinner," a mother says to her daughter's back as the youngster vanishes from the kitchen.

"Nobody can make me do what I don't want to do," she says to herself. It's her way of saying no to her parents. She feels a rush of triumph.

The power shifts from parent to child. In many ways the now-defiant and stubborn anorexic is calling the shots. At a minimum, she has their attention. She is in control.

Now she controls not only the food she eats but also many parts of her life. She may be enjoying the newfound power she has over her parents. She feels confident when she's losing weight, worthless when she's not.

Meanwhile she hoards food in secret places. She endlessly studies jar labels, content lists, what foods are good for her, what foods are bad. She can discuss nutrition, vitamins, the value of protein, how much fat is in a graham cracker.

She has become a walking, talking encyclopedia of food. She keeps on studying. She reads recipe books, shops for groceries, cooks for everyone but herself. She pretends she's interested in healthy eating. That's a cover-up. In fact she's edging closer to barely eating at all.

Her dreams are filled with elaborate meals.

The symptoms of anorexia begin to take their toll. Dieting to excess has dangerous consequences. Besides resembling a sack of bones, her skin and the hair on her head may be affected. Her arms and back may become covered with a fuzzy down—lanugo—that grows to protect her body and keep in the heat. She may always be cold. Her menstrual cycle—if it has started—may stop. Her kidneys may fail.

Long-term dieting is hazardous to your health. If you recognize yourself on these pages and suspect these warning signs apply to you, get help.

Danger Signs That Can Be Seen or Felt

skeletal look	fainting spells
sunken eyes	inability to sleep
dry skin, may turn yellow or gray	cold or numb hands and feet
hands and feet may turn blue	shortness of breath
hair thins on head	exhaustion
hair grows on arms, legs, and other body parts	periods stop or never start
loss of muscle and body fat	muscle cramps
tremors	frequent urge to urinate
constipation, bloating	depression, anxiety

Unseen Dangers

shrunken heart, irregular beat	low blood pressure, slower pulse
low body temperature	thyroid function slows
bone mineral loss, brittle bones	growth stunted

Queen of the World

A person with anorexia often exercises a lot. Aerobics a half hour at a time five times a day. Six times a week for an hour. Every single day for as long as possible. She's afraid she'll gain weight if she doesn't keep moving.

So she doesn't stop. She exercises to the point of exhaustion. Now in addition to all of the other possible problems related to not eating right, she runs the risk of torn muscles, torn ligaments, and stress fractures. She doesn't care. She refuses to be distracted.

Her goal is to be better at her exercise program than anyone else. She will master it. She should star in her own video. She *will* keep off the fat.

DEATH'S DOOR

Of those hospitalized for the treatment of anorexia, 38 percent relapse within two years of getting better and have to be hospitalized again.[2]

Constant motion, starvation, food rituals, isolation—this is the life of the anorexic. She thinks, "I'm in control here. I'm not hurting anybody, so people should just leave me alone." Being skinny makes her feel like the Queen of the World.

She never sees how thin she is. She only worries how fat she is. The eating disorder has become her identity. She thinks it makes her special. If she were not an anorexic, she would be nothing at all. Less than nothing. Is it any wonder she's terrified to quit?

Fierce and Committed Warrior

"Not eating is all I've got," she says to herself. And she's good at it. The hunger drive is a powerful one. She's defying it, like a fierce and committed warrior. Sometimes, though, she makes herself so hungry, she can't keep that iron-fisted control.

She eats.

She eats.

She eats.

She purges. She rids herself of the food in her body.

She hates herself. Once again she exerts her amazing control. She returns to starving herself despite the fact that the praise and compliments long ago stopped. Now people whisper behind her back. They call her new names, like Skeleton and Bone Brain. They tell her she's crazy, a wacko. They confront her, point-blank, and ask, "Are you anorexic?"

"Of course not," she says, denying the truth to herself as well as to others. She's crafting a new talent: lying. She lies to her friends. She lies to her parents.

Her mother asks, "Did you eat today?"

"Sure," she answers, knowing she only had a single bite of a dry sandwich and two sips of a diet soda.

Her friends beg her, plead with her, push her to eat until their faces are as blue as her hands and feet may be turning. Her heart may be beating erratically. She may feel bloated, as if she's swallowed an inflated balloon. Still she tells those who question her, "Nothing is wrong."

Or, depending on her mood at the moment, she tells them it's none of their business.

Or she gives them excuses: "Oh, I have the flu, a cold, an upset stomach," whatever ailment pops into her head.

She thinks, "They're jealous. They don't have the willpower that I do." She feels an exciting sense of control. It makes her feel superior to others. And superior people are entitled to lie.

"No more food for me," she says. "I'm full."

She stares in the mirror, but the visual reality doesn't register in her brain. She is incapable of seeing what others see. Her eyes skip over their dark circles, her hollow cheeks, hunched shoulders, sunken chest, bony elbows, scrawny legs, and knobby knees. Instead they focus on what she's convinced is a still-remaining layer of fat, right there, on her hips and on her belly.

Experts have a name for this symptom: distorted self-image. And it's universal. No person with anorexia, even if she is near death from self-starvation, ever believes she is sufficiently thin. In fact, she worries that the opposite is true.

Like a stuck CD, she asks over and over, "Do you think I'm too fat? Do you think I'm too fat?"

Civil War

A person with anorexia worries so much that she's still overweight that her mood swings as her emotions go back and forth. She no longer casts herself as the Queen of the World. She's the lowest of the low, a commoner with the self-esteem of a flea.

Suddenly it's as if a

DEATH SENTENCE

Experts estimate that between 10 percent and 20 percent of those with anorexia die from it.[3]

THE FIRST RECORDED DEATH

What is now known as anorexia was first described in medical literature three centuries ago. The symptoms were the same then as they are today. The case was a female whose eating patterns changed when she was eighteen. By twenty, she had died of this condition.[4]

civil war is raging inside her head. One minute she feels above everybody, 100 percent in control. Then comes a chilling crash. She feels worthless.

It's horrifying.

She almost goes into a trance. A voice tells her she's inadequate. Inferior. Despised by others. Her friends and family think she's a joke. They look down on her, disapprove of her, are quick to find fault.

"Aren't they always screaming at me about my diet?" she thinks to herself, gathering proof.

A voice tells her she does everything wrong. She must punish herself, cut herself, burn herself. She doesn't deserve to live. She should commit slow suicide.

"They want me out of their lives?" she thinks. "They want to reject me? Well, I'll dump them first." She eats so little she'll disappear. She will no longer have a body.

"I'll show them," she thinks, and she thinks about death.

Anorexia takes her whole mind and every part of her body and destroys them. Anorexia is an eating disorder that eats a person alive.

hungry
heart

Nothing's Wrong

Anne, age twelve: If anybody sees me, they'd think nothing is wrong. But they'd be wrong. I have a secret that is breaking my heart: I don't like to eat in front of my friends, because afterward I throw up. Only one person knows this; I'll tell you about that in a minute.

I was in fifth grade when I started to throw up. I did it on and off in sixth grade, too. Then I started again this past summer before seventh grade. No one but me was home during the day. I ate a lot—I mean a real lot. Like, I was a peanut-butter monster. I could finish a big jar in one sitting. I could eat two family-size boxes of cereal.

Once I was eating a 2,000-calorie sandwich when a neighbor stopped by with a box of Dunkin' Donuts. I began popping them into my mouth. "What is it with this eating thing?" I wondered.

At least I wasn't stealing food or taking it from some-body else's refrigerator. But the problem was when I ate like that I would feel bad and guilty the rest of the day. Plus I got chubby.

Once school started, I'd be walking down the hall and I could hear people saying to me, "Hey, Fat Girl." I was playing sports and had good friends, but none of that mattered. I was so hurt by those words.

First I tried to work out to lose some weight. I lost about twenty pounds. But the words kept haunting me. I thought if I started to throw up again, I could be thin again.

So that's what I've been doing. My best friend, Deirdre, said, "Wow, tell me about your diet." I wanted to tell her the truth, but I couldn't. I knew she'd tell my dad and he'd go crazy.

No one found out what I was doing until about a month ago. It was a day when I was just soooo hungry I couldn't help myself. I ate some lunch at school and felt uncomfortable. I thought I could sneak off to a bathroom that no one used much. I didn't know Deirdre was following me.

When she came into the bathroom and heard me throw-ing up, she started banging on the door. Since I was in such a hurry, I didn't lock it right and the door swung open. Deirdre tried to stop me, but it was too late.

She slapped me across the face and said, "What are you doing?" I couldn't keep the secret from her any longer. And once I told her, I felt a little better. I told her the real reasons, too.

Everything's Wrong

I do it because my parents are divorced and Katherine, my mom, wants to be back in my life after four years.

I do it because I'm having trouble in school for the first time ever.

I do it because my longtime boyfriend and I have been having fights over small things.

I do it because a guy I was fooling around with is going out with someone else, but he tells Deirdre that he still has feelings for me.

"How long have you been doing this?" she asks.

"Off and on for two years," I say. I don't tell her that lately I've been throwing up blood. "Please, please, you just can't tell anyone," I say to her.

I don't know exactly what the problem I have is called, but I would like to find out more about it and try to help other young people with problems like I have. Right now I take one day at a time. But I still throw up after I eat. It makes me feel cleansed. Now I do it after every single meal.

chapter 5

yum, yum, yum, barf

Closet Eater

Bulimia.

The hunger drive is a powerful one.

The anorexic defies it.

The person with bulimia surrenders to it. She hides from others and secretly eats.

Hers becomes an all-or-nothing approach to food. Once she goes ahead and takes that first bite, she immediately worries, "I've blown it. How can I diet today? I'll start tomorrow."

For now, though, it's on to the entire Sara Lee cheese-cake, still half frozen. It disappears as if by magic. Then she stuffs down other favorites, or if necessary, whatever else is around: burritos, lasagna, fruit, sandwiches.

She prefers sweet stuff, fatty stuff, chocolate bars, ice cream, and cookies—food that fills her up, food that brings her comfort. These are hand-to-mouth bingeing sessions, where her movements become automatic, unthinking—like a machine.

She eats until she can hardly move. She eats until she's in physical pain. When she's done, she picks up the wrappers, the boxes, the containers. She works to get rid of the evidence. Some she tucks away in her pockets, others in corners of her room, in her dresser drawers. Wherever.

Black Sheep

She knows she keeps eating when she's no longer hungry. In fact, hunger has little to do with what happens. She eats for other reasons. It's an impulse that hits her.

In her mind, she walks the halls of school all alone. She wants to have friends, but . . . friends might be back-stabbers. Friends might betray her.

She's afraid to put down her mask and let others peer in. If they know the real her, she's afraid they won't like her. Or at least, they'll discover the truth. She's a loser.

She'd give anything to be popular, to look like Megan or Jasmine, Amber or Kate.

She believes that her life, along with her emotions, is a mess. At the darkest moments, she thinks about suicide. If the anorexic wants to be a fragile little girl, the bulimic wants to be the perfect, successful young lady. But she fears that she's the black sheep of the family. Whether it's real or imagined, she feels she's always in trouble and is not even sure why.

It's as if her parents issued a set of rules without remembering to give her a copy. At home she doesn't know what is right or what is wrong. What gets punished and what doesn't. What is enough and what is too much.

***

Soothing the Pain

Experts say that the person with bulimia eats because she hurts emotionally and doesn't know how to handle it. She eats because she can't make sense of the world around her.

She eats when she feels left out. She eats when she's confronted by change. She eats when she gets a bad grade. She eats when she wants to block out her parents' fighting, when that certain guy in class ignores her, when she's as lonely as an alien from outer space.

Eating, she discovers, soothes her pain. It removes her angry thoughts. It makes her feel cushioned, loved, and secure. The pressure and anxiety that builds in her life is calmed by eating. She escapes all feelings during a binge. Nothing else matters. She eats and she eats and she eats—alone.

STARVE AND STUFF

Fifty percent of anorexics also are bulimics. Twenty percent of bulimics have anorexic periods.[5]

This is part of her secret life. She doesn't want others to know what she's doing. In the school cafeteria, at McDonald's, at the family table, she never binges. She nibbles or eats as much as her friends eat.

She knows that only boys can get away with gorging in public on too many hamburgers. People think that's funny. They think it's okay. Boys can even have contests to see who can put away the most pizza, hot dogs, potato chips.

Catch a girl doing the same thing, forget it. People shake their heads and let her know they think her behavior is unacceptable. A girl is supposed to be nice and feminine.

Greedy, Needy, and Disgusting

A bulimic has been taught to be ashamed if she makes a mess. But she likes to do it, even when she's the only one who knows it. For the length of a binge, it's fun to be greedy, needy, and disgusting.

She knows that in real life her parents would be upset. But when she's by herself she can eat with her hands, both hands. If she wants to, she can smear the food on her face in her race to eat as much as possible as fast as she can. She can secretly misbehave.

Food has become her life. When she eats like this, she no longer feels nervous, depressed, or bored. It's her guard against feeling rejected. She's not like the anorexic who has two crackers and an olive and calls it dinner. Food is her friend, until the binge is over. Then it's her enemy. She hates it. She curses herself for every bite she's taken.

STOPPING/STARTING A BINGE

Some bulimics try different ways to keep from bingeing. They hide food from themselves, pour detergent in it, lock it away. But none of that matters. When they want to binge, there is no stopping them.

Some only binge on weekends. Some binge daily. Some binge on certain forbidden foods. Some eat one meal on top of another. A binge can last for several hours or even off and on for several days.[6]

For all their differences, there are similarities that bind those with these two types of eating disorders. They both have an unreasonable fear that one day, suddenly, they'll be as big as a truck.

They both are preoccupied with the shape of their body, carry exercise to extremes, and experience tremendous mood swings. They both turn over control of their lives to the disorder, the exact opposite of what they mean to do. They both deny themselves a whole range of experiences because of food.

The anorexic doesn't want to eat. The bulimic wants to be alone in a secret place—eating.

And if the parents of a bulimic discover what is going on, she wages just as fierce a power struggle over this issue as the anorexic does.

Shame and Embarrassment

For the bulimic, when the binge is finished, her emotions return. She's ashamed of herself. She's embarrassed. How could she lose control this way? She doesn't want to be fat, and bingeing means that her daily total of calories is beyond counting.

She knows she'll gain weight. She can already feel it. She feels bad. Tomorrow, for sure, she will regain control of her life and her body by rigidly dieting.

So the next day, she tries to diet. Maybe she skips breakfast entirely, then the same with lunch. She tells herself she will fast. She'll eat nothing the whole day. But the bulimic doesn't really need to worry about dieting. She has a hidden weapon, a dark secret.

Purging: The Magic Solution

For the bulimic, all that matters is to be thin. And she has discovered a magic solution. She can have it both ways. She can eat everything she wants without getting fat. How she does this is her other well-kept secret, and her other shame.

She purges.

Many a bulimic believes she is the only one to stumble on this method of undoing binges. She thinks she invented it. For others, it's common knowledge.

Girlfriends get together and show each other how to do it. Their mothers, and maybe even their grand-mothers, have known about bingeing and purging since their own youth.

The behavior patterns of a bulimic are often harder to detect than those of an anorexic. A bulimic rarely ends up with the same skeletal look. More often she's close to normal weight for her height and age, give or take ten to fifteen pounds.

Why? Because after eating, she heads for the bathroom. She uses one or several ways to rid herself of what she eats.

A RELATED DISORDER: THE COMPULSIVE OVEREATER

Draw a horizontal line across a blank sheet of paper. On one side write the word "anorexic." On the other side write "compulsive overeater."* In the middle, write "bulimic."

These three eating disorders are related. Those who use food as an escape from dealing with life's problems share various characteristics. At different times they may even move back and forth among these eating patterns.

As with a bulimic, a compulsive overeater goes on secret, uncontrollable binges. She eats because food is love, a reward, a tranquilizer. She eats when she's not physically hungry; then she feels she's bad. She knows her eating

She might teach herself to throw up. At first it's not as simple as she'd like to believe. It takes practice. It can be painful. But it does bring about the desired result. And eventually she gets good at it.

Why not have three slices of pie, if she knows it will no longer count in her daily calorie total.

When this purging becomes frequent, she thinks about the lingering smell and the sound of it. She takes care to hide the evidence. She opens the window. She sprays different fragrances. She turns on the faucet, the radio, the shower, to muffle the noise.

The frequency of purging varies from person to person. She ignores the fact that even if it's once a week, it's a dangerous habit. She may not die from starvation the way a girl with anorexia could, but she can ruin her health and sign her own death warrant because of her risky actions.

behavior isn't typical, but she tells herself she can't help it. She has no willpower at all.

She goes on diets, lots of them, losing and gaining those same pounds. She gets depressed. She bases her successes and failures on her weight.

Depending on which source is used, between 10 percent and 40 percent of obese people may be binge eaters. But they don't take the next step that bulimics do. They don't make up for their overeating by purging, fasting, or fanatically exercising.[7]

*Binge eating disorder is another name for compulsive overeating.

The Challenge

In her relentless pursuit of thinness, the bulimic might start using laxatives, water pills, diet pills, enemas, whatever she can get her hands on to reinforce her feeling of control. While she'd like to believe all these methods help her lose weight, they don't really. Instead they can even cause bloating, which helps convince her she's fatter than she is.

She starts to challenge herself about the amount her body can handle. Can she take a half package of laxatives today? What about a whole package?

How many of those other pills can she use in a day? Five? Fifty? One hundred fifty? Two hundred?

An anorexic is structured and rigid. The bulimic lives wild, in-and-out-of-control cycles of bingeing and purging which become her routine. They are her rituals. They give her life its rhythm.

She may arrange the order of the food she'll eat. She may have exact situations and ways to purge—after her piano lessons, when she's finished her homework, late at night when everybody else is sleeping. She may mark on a calendar the number of times she purges. The more marks she sees, the better she feels. Some days she'll eat just so she can purge and mark it down.

"If I don't do that," she thinks to herself, "I feel something is missing."

Still she's in a constant battle with herself over when to binge. There are good days and bad days; good days when she doesn't binge, bad days when the bingeing takes over.

To purge, in her mind, is to regain control. It is purifying.

Some experts believe that purging acts like a narcotic and gives her a rush, similar to a runner's high. The bingeing and purging are addictive. Together they're as powerful as the anorexic's self-starvation.

There's no way she can easily give them up. She grows to

RED ALERT

Long-term bingeing and purging are hazardous to your health. If you recognize yourself on these pages and suspect these warning signs apply to you, get help.

Danger Signs That Can Be Seen or Felt

vomiting blood	muscle weakness
tooth decay, loss of enamel	mood swings, depression
swollen glands in neck	exhaustion
broken blood vessels in face	abdominal pain, cramps
blurred vision	sore throat
dry, flaky skin	indigestion
bloating	water retention
periods stop or never start	constipation

Unseen Dangers

body's fluid and mineral balance upset (electrolyte imbalance)	damage to bowels, liver, and kidney
dehydration	heart attack

love these feelings of ela-
tion more than anything.

Emergency Room

The younger the bulim-
ic, the more serious the
medical consequences.
Bingeing, purging, fast-

THE SECRET CONDITION

Before 1940 there was hardly any information about bulimia in medical literature. It was seen as part of anorexia.
Since 1979-80, it has been described as
a separate condition.[10]

ing, dieting, and overexercising can upset the entire body
and every organ in it.

Her body's in a period of rapid growth. All of these
things can retard it. Throwing up repeatedly can eat the
enamel right off her teeth. Her heart can be affected; it
might race or skip beats. There can be kidney damage; she
won't be able to make urine and rid her body of waste.

Her brain, her thoughts, her moods can be affected. She
might collapse and even lose consciousness.

Still she might think, "Big deal. Besides, it can't happen
to me." And then she finds herself in a hospital emergency
room. Her parents have learned her secret and a doctor is
recommending treatment.

chapter 6

digesting the facts

Ask the Experts

Why would people let an eating disorder ruin their lives? Why would they practice the eating patterns described in chapters three and five?

Ask those questions of specialists, physicians, therapists, representatives of organizations concerned with this issue— then stand back for the uproar. That's the sound of their voices as they agree and disagree about the causes and cures.

Some experts say the seeds are planted almost at birth. Children as young as two years old want to be thin. How do we know? Researchers show them silhouettes and dolls of different sizes. "Which of these dolls has the most friends?" the researchers ask. "The thin ones do," comes their answer.[11]

They mix in dolls with physical disabilities, dolls of different skin colors, and ask more questions.

Disabilities and skin color don't matter to little kids, but thin and heavy do. The only creatures in their lives allowed to be soft and round and remain popular are teddy bears and characters in cartoons.

By the time girls and boys turn five and six, they've learned to feel self-conscious about their looks. Chunky kids get teased and tormented. They're supposed to laugh at stories about fat people getting stuck in doorways.[12]

Some youngsters are already being pushed by their parents to watch what they eat. The girls are bothered by their weight; boys care more about height.

Once they're seven, eight, and nine years old, children tell researchers flat out they don't like fat bodies. They have decided that heavier people are lazy, liars, and cheaters. They have learned that from the adult world that surrounds them.[13]

100 Percent Perfect Message

Why do younger and younger people feel pressure to be thin? First let's consider something we'll call the message. It can start with those flashy supermodels, the ones with the amazingly skinny bodies. They look you in the eye as they stare from magazine pages and oversize billboards.

The hot TV and movie stars reinforce the same theme, but with an added twist. Today you have to be thin *and* buff, a body with fantastic mini-muscles and a flat-flat stomach.

The message is: Be sexy, be cool, be in shape, and above everything, be lean. There is no room for hippo thighs, no room for bellies with more rolls than a bakery, no room for second chins. Just 100 percent perfect bodies.

Day in and day out, coming at you from all directions,

they speak to you this silent message: Fat is ugly. Thin is beautiful. The message repeats and repeats until those perfect bodies become so much a part of your life, you start to believe that their shape is the only one acceptable. And, of course, desirable. Anybody whose bones are covered with more than a little skin must be . . . fat. And fat is ugly.

Mission accomplished.

You have learned the message by heart.

Aargh

Now here's a problem. You look in the mirror and you don't see anybody who could be mistaken for this year's Miss America. You see *you*. "Aargh," you think. "I'm not thin."

The message wouldn't matter so much if it didn't come with a second part. Many of you take this next step. You come to believe a faulty logic.

What difference does it make if you believe that logic? Plenty. For starters, it puts you in a dangerous state of mind. For girls and boys about to become women and men, the message gets mixed in with all the other changes and challenges going on in your life.

The ingredients are falling into place, ingredients that can mix together to create an eating disorder.

FAULTY LOGIC

You say to yourself, "Thin, beautiful people are always smiling. They have fun and are fun to be with. They don't have any real problems."

You say to yourself, "Thin, beautiful people have it made. They're in control of their lives."

You say to yourself, "If I want to be successful like them, I have to be thin."

You say to yourself, "If I'm thin, people will like me more. I'll be everything I ever wanted to be."

***

Body Torment

Picture a room full of girls ranging in age from eight to twelve. They are short and round, tall and thin, big and bony. Some have bodies you envy. Some don't. They are all different.

All the girls are growing up, leading lives in transition. They are going through physical and emotional changes. In fact, they will be going through them for some years to come.

The changes in their bodies torment them. They're no dummies. They're convinced that in our society, they're being evaluated mainly by how they look. They have just got to be attractive.

BAD BODY PARTS

I hate my body. I cannot fit into a two-piece bathing suit without wanting to hide. You see, there's my figure. What figure? I don't have a single curve. It goes straight down.

My parents say I have a beautiful body, but I'm their daughter. That's what they're supposed to say. My friends say I have a nice body; I should accept the way I am and get on with my life.

—Tammy, age thirteen

But they're growing round in the wrong places, and it's all happening too fast. Or they're not growing round in the right places, and a few muscles would be nice.

They study their image. They're obsessed with their shape. And just when some curves appear, they remember the message: Thin is beautiful. If asked, they would tell you exactly how they feel about their body. They hate it—all of it, or at least in parts.

Weird Changes

In addition to concern over physical changes, the changes in personality and emotions are also troubling. Something weird happens to girls as they enter their adolescent years. Before that time they seem ready for everything, from climbing a mountain to baking a pie.

They have courage and boldness and are proud of those characteristics. Then around the ages of eleven, twelve, or thirteen, inside their heads they hear society's messages far more clearly. Forget that wild little girl, they hear. Forget her and turn into . . . what? They don't really know how to answer that question.

Some girls have no idea how to behave in these years of transition. They feel as if they went to sleep in their own secure room and woke up in a foreign country.

There's a new way of talking, a new way of walking. Out of the blue they're supposed to know how to move their body so it makes the opposite sex sit up and take notice. And that scares them, too. They already know about date rape, unplanned babies, and sexually transmitted diseases, including AIDS.

MORE BAD BODY PARTS

I hate that I have more freckles than sand on a beach.
—Suzannah, age nine

I hate my rat's-nest hair.
—Tiffany, age ten

I hate my lips. When my friends and I kiss paper with lipstick on, I'm embarrassed.
—Carrie, age eight

I hate my Miss Piggy nose. All my friends have cute button ones. Is there a plastic surgeon in the house?
—Lilly, age eleven

One day they feel fine. The next day they're a wreck. One day they feel ready to conquer the globe. The next day they worry, will they look like a dork if they wear green plaid socks? They are bewildered. Too many of them lose their joyous optimism. They become less curious and less likely to take risks.

Adolescent girls start to live their lives as if they're in the middle of a minefield. And in many ways, they are. They become cautious.

Some girls do test their boundaries. They explore, but in a different way than they used to. The world beyond their front doors can be forbidding. So they argue with their parents instead. Parents naturally want to protect them. The girls begin to rebel.

These two different goals come into conflict. The girls claim they aren't allowed to be themselves. Confident, well-adjusted nine-year-olds are turning into sad and angry twelve-year-olds. Their parents don't know what to do to stop it. It alarms them and breaks their hearts at the same time. They demand their daughters toss out favorite CDs, posters, and magazines. They're bad influences.

These girls begin to have secrets. They focus on themselves.

Privacy becomes an important issue.

They get the moody blues.

"Where were you until so late?" parents demand to know.

"With friends" is the reply. Parents want details, all of them, immediately. Parents see freedom as risky business, and they're right.

These girls, whether they're brave or frightened, don't understand all these troubling things that are happening to them. It's almost as if they've become different people.

But it's society—not their parents—that is pressuring them to forget who they are and their full range of talents.

They believe they're expected to turn into some kind of a replacement person, a shadow of the girl they're leaving behind.

The closer they get to their teen years, the more they begin to shut down. They lose their strong sense of adventure. They lose their boldness.

STILL MORE BAD BODY PARTS

I hate my stomach—not the organ, but the outside appearance. It could definitely use some trimming. I've always wanted a really tight stomach, but I've never been able to just jump in head-first and commit to a diet. I try, but it's my version of a diet.

Sometimes I don't understand how all the girls on TV are so skinny and maintain that look. I can't even achieve it, let alone maintain it. Long fingernails would be nice, too, and thirteen holes in each ear and bigger, darker brown eyes. —Alicia, age eleven

I hate my oversized butt. My friends and family always joke, "With a butt like that you won't need a cushion for the chair." It hurts to hear that.

My mom tells me when she was younger, she used to have a big butt, too. "It's not easy," she says. In the future I hope they come up with a butt-decrease operation.

—Haley, age thirteen

They don't think they're popular. They don't think they're as smart as they really are. They set themselves up to believe that they are failures, when in fact, they aren't.

Too many of them feel like zeroes.

Peer Pressure

Adolescence, the time of separation, used to begin around the ages of twelve, thirteen, or fourteen. Today it's not unusual for kids far younger to be thinking about breaking away. They're preparing and plotting. They're getting set to issue their declaration of independence.

They feel an enormous pressure to fit in. They wish for real friends, friends who are always there for them. They wish for friends they can talk to about anything. But adolescents can be mean and vicious to one another. They know how to inflict pain. It's hard to know who to trust.

Girls this age also make decisions based on the popular values of the moment. Their parents' opinions just don't matter in the same way. On cold winter mornings they blow out their breath to pretend they're smoking. Smoking, they think, is cool. It's grown-up. They go to school carrying low-fat food. "Don't you know, I'm totally overweight," they say to their friends.

Overgeneralizing is another characteristic of this age. There is only black and white. There are no shades of gray. They tell their mothers, "Everyone in my class is on a diet." (Well, almost everyone. The only ones who aren't are those who are skinny naturally. That doesn't count. They're called the toothpicks, the beanpoles, the razor blades.)

EVEN MORE BAD BODY PARTS

At school I see so many people with perfect bodies. I'm not one of them. I know that being overweight is a problem, but being underweight is, too. I'm in seventh grade and I only weigh seventy pounds. Some people even think I am anorexic.

They're wrong. This is the way I am. People make fun of me because I'm skinny when I don't want to be. They are always bugging me about it. Sometimes I feel like I CAN'T STAND IT ANYMORE!!!
—Maria, age twelve

A few generations ago, girls didn't start to menstruate until they were about fifteen or sixteen. Now with each passing decade, the age drops lower. Today having started their period can be a topic of conversation among girls in fifth and sixth grade. They find out the truth in school rest rooms, at home over the phone, or at sleep-overs, where as little sleep as possible takes place.

They learn there's a kind of dividing line between those who have gotten "it" and those who haven't. There's a related dividing line between those who are beginning to date and those who can't imagine doing anything so silly.

Low-Fat Milk and Diet Pills

The correct appearance has always been important. Now it takes more money to achieve it. There is designer makeup and designer clothes. Little girls play at painting their nails. Then one day they start wearing lip liner and gloss for real. They dress in styles that don't look all that different from what their older sisters wear: Calvin Klein this, Patagonia that, and just the right shoes.

BOYS WORRY, TOO

If there was one thing I'd change about my looks, I'd change my weight. I get poked at and yelled at all the time. I'd like to be mostly skinny instead of fat.

Then I wouldn't be teased anymore, and I'd be able to do things I can't do now. I could run faster and be more active. I could swim, knowing I don't have all that weight on me.

—Mike, age ten

Today most girls can talk about cholesterol and the benefits of low-fat milk. At the drugstore they join their peers in front of rows of diet pills, Dexatrim, and Fibertrim. The big fear in this world they're entering is weight.

They worry.

They've heard it often enough, one way or another. They won't be given time to show all that they have to offer. First impressions will be the lasting impressions.

Aargh.

✳✳✳

Mirror Time

What about boys this age, between eight and twelve? Doesn't heading into adolescence ever make them feel crazy? They're leading lives in transition, too. Don't they worry about the size and the shape of their bodies?

Of course.

But still the experts say facts are facts. Eighty-five to 90 percent of those with eating disorders are female. But what about that 10 to 15 percent? Many boys that age—and especially a couple of years older—are having problems, too. They feel weird and insecure. They don't want to admit that they care how they look. They put in plenty of mirror time, but they disguise it.

They think an eating disorder is a girl thing, and they don't want to talk about it.

All it means is this: If boys do become anorexic or bulimic, it's less likely to be noticed. They're also far less likely to actively look for help.

Boys want to fit in as much as girls do. Most of them just don't feel the same pressure to be thin. For them there's a competing American image: the humongous jock. If they don't have to keep their weight down to be successful long-

EGGS ONLY

My brother, Chad, stopped eating right when he was ten. At the time he was going to a private boarding school. Months went by and when we'd go up there to take him out to eat, we thought it was weird. He'd just order eggs and only eat half of them. Before that he'd eat everything in sight.

By then he'd become moody, too, always in a hurry to get back to the dorm or get off the phone with my parents. He lost thirty pounds, dropping from one hundred to seventy. At four feet nine inches, that was too little.

My parents freaked. They couldn't

distance runners, wrestlers, or swimmers, if they don't want to be lean and mean, they sure wouldn't mind being bigger, heavier, and stronger.

A monster. A good big man will always beat a good little man.

They already know about lifting weights and working out. Some of them have exercise schedules. Today boys—and girls—often live in homes where Stair-Masters and other exercise machines are part of the furniture. They know the benefit of the aerobic rider. On it they can exercise both the upper and lower body. They know about doing the exercise circuit, about pecs and abs, and the best workout videos.

believe no one at the school saw it as a problem. They wondered, maybe the school was the problem. They pulled him out.

At home they'd try to talk to him. They'd say, "You can die from anorexia." Chad would walk away. Lately, though, he seems to be getting better. No one knows exactly what happened, but as my dad says, "Leave well enough alone."

He may be right. All Chad would say to me is he's one of the few lucky people who get healed from this disease. Still, I worry.

—Pearl, age twelve

Normal-Looking Human Beings

Male or female, no matter whether they feel like a little kid or an almost-teenager, adolescents look in the mirror and know what they see. Themselves. A pretty normal-looking human being.

Some say, "So what," and go about their business. Some cry and want to do something about it. But what?

They could lose weight. Thin is beautiful.

* * *

Your Next Birthday

Different experts report having seen girls and boys as young as seven and eight with eating disorders. It's no longer unusual for nine-, ten-, and eleven-year-olds to be sent to professionals for help.

The peak ages for the symptoms of anorexia to show up are twelve to thirteen and again at seventeen—times of transition.[14] With bulimia there's disagreement. Some experts say that it usually starts somewhere in the late teens or early twenties, and it's possible to develop it in the thirties, forties, and even fifties.[15] Other experts say, "Wrong. Bulimia, too, can develop around twelve to thirteen."[16]

Regardless of the exact age when eating disorders start, one fact remains. The age of those at risk is dropping. This means your riskiest time could be as close as your next birthday.

SHAMU THE WHALE

I hate my entire appearance. My hair is too thin, and I wish it was curly. I hate my face. My ears stick out, and now I have acne. But the worst is my weight. I eat little during the week, six hundred calories a day. On weekends I binge majorly. I can't stop thinking about food. I am fat. I am disgusting.

At school they call me Shamu the Whale. I try to laugh with them. Inside I cry. I've tried Weight Watchers, a swim class, a nutrition therapist. I've been on a diet since I was eight.

—Brittany, age ten

life out of balance

Boxed in and Overloaded

Just living through preadolescence can throw kids out of balance. Then add to that the fact that many girls and boys are boxed in by adult-size personal and family problems. They go on emotional overload.

Which gets us back to eating disorders.

Experts agree that eating disorders don't spring from a single cause. Instead they grow from just such an overload of troubles. Each one by itself is a risk factor. Stack up enough of them, and together they spell danger.

Introductions

Meet Shannon and Emily. Shannon is eleven years old and Emily, twelve. They go to two different middle schools on opposite coasts. They both like their classes and try hard to excel.

They are involved in other activities as well. Shannon plays the clarinet in the school band, and Emily sings in her church choir.

Shannon and Emily have both had personal experiences with eating disorders. Both got dangerously close to having an eating disorder run their lives. Emily is still in trouble.

Their stories could remind you of others you know. They could remind you of no one you've ever met. They could remind you of you.

Shannon goes first.

Shannon's Real-Life Story

I was eight. What I remember is that a month into school, around October, I just stopped eating anything that wasn't liquid.

My mom would make noodle soup. She'd say, "Shannon, eat the noodles. They're soft. They'll just glide down your throat."

I'd try to, but I didn't feel comfortable eating.

"No, Mom," I said. "I don't feel like it."

I drained the soup and drank only the broth. I took a thermos to school.

I don't remember why or how I started to do that. I think it was something that came from the secret part of my mind, my subconscious. It's not like one day I sat down and said to myself, "From today on, it's only liquids for me."

A week went by, two weeks, three. I started to feel weird. I got horrible diarrhea. I felt kind of tired all the time. Without solid food, there wasn't much nutrition going on in my body.

At first I don't think my mom was that worried. She thought it was a phase. By Thanksgiving, though, when we went to my uncle Dave's, that's another story.

My mom and I have always been close. I love her a lot. I could tell she was scared. She couldn't figure out what was going on.

She said, "Are you depressed about something, and that's why you're not eating? Do you want to see a doctor?"

"No," I told her.

"I know you're not a real picky eater," she said. "But I have told you that if you don't eat your spinach, you don't get dessert. Are we in a food fight?"

"No," I told her.

I was at a new school and didn't really have a best friend. She wanted to know if that was bothering me.

"No," I told her.

I have a learning disorder, but what else is new? She wanted to know if going to a counselor about that was bothering me.

"No," I told her. "And I don't think I'm looking for attention. I'm just doing what I want to do. My mind says, 'Forget food.' That's it. Nothing else is going on."

We were at Uncle Dave's for a week, and all I ate was tomato soup. I tried to eat mashed potatoes on Thanksgiving Day, but I couldn't take it. They'd try to get me to eat by putting food in front of me. They'd eat and talk about how good the food was.

By then I was in pain. The only time I felt okay was when I was asleep. Next I got seriously constipated. It was such a change for my body to go through.

My mom said, "Shannon, if you keep this up, you could die."

I figured, no way. That wasn't anything that happened to little girls like me.

❊❊❊

Once we were home, I could hear my mom on the phone long-distance with my father. "Shannon's on a hunger strike," she said. "I think it's because she hasn't seen you for a long time. You are her father. She needs you in her life."

My parents got divorced when I was four. My dad remarried by the time I was five. When I was seven, he officially adopted my stepmom's son. I tried to explain to myself why that was okay. Why that shouldn't hurt my feelings.

This whole time, I don't know if I knew for sure that I missed my father. Was he even someone who should have been there, at least every now and then? I did know that sometimes I envied kids who were sent between their divorced parents' homes like pieces of mail.

My mom put me on the phone. "I'm in a play." I told my dad.

"I'll try to come to see you," he said. And he did.

The day before he arrived, my mom picked me up after school. She told me the news, and when we got home, I said, "I'm hungry." She had gotten a salad. I hated cucumbers, but I ate a little bit of them anyway. Little by little I started to eat again. It took my body a long time to get used to solid food. I think it was glad, though, to get back to normal.

When my dad showed up, he wondered why I quit eating. But mainly, it's not too great to talk about, and everyone seemed to want to avoid it.

Now that I'm older, I think it was a pretty crazy thing to do. I think I was depressed about my father and didn't realize it. I was too little to figure out what was bothering me.

Since this summer, I have thought about diets. I've tried some, too. But mainly I listen to Richard Simmons, the diet guy who wears shorts and a tank top and hugs people. He says diets are not going to do anything if you don't exercise.

So now I'm exercising and feeling fine. Crunches, which are quarter sit-ups, are my favorites. They're totally amazing.

Emily's Real-Life Story

You could say I had a normal appetite until my mom remarried. That was a year or so ago. I don't understand how she can stand to be with him. He's so ugly.

Sometimes I wonder, did she marry him for me? He's a doctor, so I suppose people would think he was nice.

But he isn't that nice to me. But then sometimes he is. It gets confusing.

Anyway, after their wedding I start to overeat. In the beginning I guess I do it out of anger about the whole situation. Things are really tense around the house.

Like, my stepfather makes these so-called jokes about charging me rent, and that I'll probably still eat more than I can pay him.

Ha-ha. I'm supposed to laugh? I think my mom should tell him, "That's not funny." But she doesn't.

Then I get a massive case of acne. My stepfather the doctor stockpiles food but starts putting me on all these restrictive diets. Meanwhile, I'm thinking, "Pass me a Twinkie."

When nobody's around, I stuff in as much as I can of my favorite foods—butterscotch sundaes, chocolate fudge cake, a box of jelly doughnuts. I become a food expert. I keep track of everything that goes into my mouth, every calorie and gram of fat.

Every weekend I go to my dad's. My time over there is no bed of roses, either. Now he's married to a woman named Mirinda. She looks like she could be a model, and to go along with that, she's always on a diet.

My dad tells me. "Fat people are disgusting. Be thin. Be beautiful. Mirinda will teach you how to diet." So I diet with Mirinda, and I sneak extra food when I'm alone.

Once I get back home. I feel like I'm breaking out of prison. I eat everything in sight. Sometimes I eat until I can't fit in any more food. Then I wait awhile and start eating again.

It's like I try to have this Food Plan for the Day. That plan is on a clean piece of paper. Then plop. I drop some snack on the paper. I crumple it up and throw it away. So much for that day's diet plan.

I don't want to overeat. I mean, who wants to sit down and have a gallon of Häagen-Dazs ice cream? But once I eat more than I think I should, I give up. Ten thousand calories later I hate myself. I wish I hadn't done that. But I have.

I read in a magazine about a girl that eats so much her stomach bursts. I'm terrified. I go to my stepfather and tell him the story. "What can people do so this won't happen?" I ask him.

"Take laxatives," he says.

How am I to know that adults don't always give you the right information? How am I to know that maybe it's his idea of a joke? Instead, I just think, "I'll try that trick."

It works. I can eat all I want and not worry about my stomach exploding.

Then I remember another trick. After school when I'm sitting in my room having finished a box of M&M's, I feel sick. I go in the bathroom.

I know what I'm doing. I've heard older girls talk about this. For all I know, Mirinda does it, too.

I pull my hair back and face the toilet. I throw up. Wow, I feel good. I can control this, not like laxatives. I never know when they'll hit.

I wait a week and I try it again. It works. I have already lost three pounds. I know because I weigh myself every morning first thing. When I get dressed for school, I don't put on anything that is tight or short. That way nobody will notice that I'm still too heavy. But just wait.

Finally I tell my best friend, Kayla. We both sit on my bed and start to cry. She keeps asking me, "Why do you do it? Why?"

I tell her different reasons. I tell her no reasons that matter. "I want to look beautiful," I say. "I want to be skinny."

"But what else?" she asks. "Are you worried that no guy will like you? They're mostly jerks, anyway."

"I'm having trouble with my parents," I say. "All of them."

Kayla says, "I want to help you, but I don't know how."

"All you can do is be there for me."

I can't tell her that by now I throw up after every dinner. I can't tell her how much I really eat or that I'm trying to stop . . . but I can't.

Risky Business

Without even reading between the lines to guess what Shannon and Emily might be leaving out, there are clues to the personal and family problems—the risk factors—in their lives.

Shannon's parents had been divorced for several years. Risk. She was missing her father. Risk. She was going to a new school. Risk. She hadn't made friends. Risk.

Emily said it herself. She was having trouble with her

parents, all four of them. That's risk times four.

Both of these girls are leading lives out of balance. They searched for ways to escape from its tension, pressure, and anxiety.

Maybe they could have escaped by shopping. Some people try to lose themselves in spending money. Maybe they could have turned to sex, drugs, or alcohol. That may be difficult for younger girls. But food is different. Food is there.

So people like Shannon and Emily end up developing eating disorders.

They use food to solve all their problems. They try to hide behind food. They convince themselves if they can control what they put in their mouth, they can overcome the problems.

But they're wrong. The problems don't go away.

At times some girls feel that they hate their parents, that their parents just don't understand them. They feel that only nerds stay close to their parents. But in their still-little-girl hearts they want Mom and Dad to be there. They want their relationships to be unchanging.

But life's not usually like that.

Divorce touches half of all families. Loved ones die. Families are forced to move. Young people have to confront these issues. What matters is not the particular situation, but how the individual responds to it.

Is there solid support—a caring adult—to turn to?

Now think about what's going on in your home. How do these risk factors compare to what's happening in your life? If any of them are similar, how are you handling them? Do you feel as if you might be at risk?

Here is a checklist of family problems that make already difficult years even harder to handle.

CHECKLIST: Life Out of Balance

Your Family	You Feel
· Parents fighting	Caught in the conflicts, wishing things could calm down.
· Parents recently divorced	Torn between grief for the missing parent and loyalty to the other.
· Single-parent home	Pressured, going from Mom's home to Dad's, parenting your parents.
· Parent recently remarried/ has new partner	Overwhelmed, entering uncharted territory of new relatives and more sets of family rules.
· Birth of sibling	Abandoned, missing the former family attention.
· Death of loved one	Dead inside, nothing can remove the sharp sense of loss.
· Family moves	Frightened, under an alien roof, separated from the familiar.
· Family illness	Confused, filling a new role with no rules to follow.
· Parent's job loss/parent returns to work	Depressed, changes in career and money matters in family upset you.
· Conflicts within family	Misunderstood, angry, and in pain.

chapter 8

recipe for trouble

The Trigger

For many girls, small events can trigger enormous reactions. They notice a diet ad with a picture of a skinny woman. They're desperate to look that way. They wake up after a night of overeating. They're devastated by what they've done. They think some guys at school are laughing about them. They break down and weep.

It comes like a bullet out of nowhere. BLAM.

The power of suggestion swings into motion. Experts call it the proximate cause, an event that triggers this conscious decision: BLAM. A diet, starting now!

Porky

She's a girl of eleven. She's always been her dad's special sweetheart. He's proud of her and her accomplishments. He watched her play a snowflake in her fourth-grade play. He cheers her on at her tennis matches.

One day he looks up from the paper as she walks by and swats her hip. "Hey," he says, "you're getting kind of porky." BLAM.

"How could he say that?" she thinks.

Maybe her dad feels nervous that she's getting some curves. With curves come male attention. He's an ex-boy. He knows about boys being interested in curves. And he doesn't like what he knows, not when it's his daughter.

What about her mom? She half smiles when her husband says that. Maybe she feels competitive. She's not so young anymore. But in the daughter's mind, her father's words make her believe: "Dad thinks I have thunder thighs. He's going to stop loving me."

And children are dependent on parents for emotional support. She decides she's got to do something about her weight right this minute. She goes on a diet.

Meatloaf

He's a boy of ten. He goes into gym class and the teacher announces they're going to measure skin folds. The idea is the skin is supposed to be tight over the bones and muscles. Not fleshy, not flabby, but tight.

The thing is, the boy just isn't built that way. He's not exactly fat, but there *is* something to measure. He's always felt self-conscious about his weight. This makes him feel worse.

All the boys in the class start hassling him. "Meatloaf," they call him. BLAM. He fights hard not to cry and he wins the fight, but he feels terrible. He doesn't know how to deal with it. He wants to be one of the guys. He doesn't want to be the class fool.

He goes home and tells his parents. He says he wants to go on a diet. They agree to help him stick to it. The next

"I tried on clothes for my cousin's wedding. I'm a size bigger than I expected."

"I went from my little elementary school down the block to a middle school with a thousand students. I feel invisible."

"My track coach tells me that to be competitive I have to lose weight."

"My boyfriend says, 'If your stomach didn't stick out so much, you'd be sexier.' Then he dumps me."

"My mom criticizes me, saying, 'A girl your age shouldn't be that heavy.'
"'Let me go to one of those exercise places,' I say.
"'No, it would be a waste of money.'
"I think to myself, 'I'll go on a diet. Maybe then there can be hope for me in the future.'"

morning he gets started. He diets.

Whatever the reason, these preteens feel down and out and imperfect. They feel out of control. The answer seems so easy. Lose weight.

Battle against the Bulge

On any given day in America, millions of people—kids and adults—begin a diet. They don't say to themselves, "Today I'm going to start to develop an eating disorder." They just want to look and feel better. It's that simple.

Early on in this battle against the bulge, how many stop to think, "I've got to diet sensibly"? How many worry, "Will I get so caught up with my diet that I won't be able to stop?"

Out of all the on-again-off-again dieters, the overeaters, the just-this-once purgers, some will end up with a full-blown eating disorder.

BLAM.

chapter 9

a mix of ingredients

What Makes the Difference?

Most people soak up the message that thin is beautiful. And most people who try to lose weight don't end up with an eating disorder.

So what makes the difference? Here comes more disagreement. In general, most experts say that it has to do with this mix of ingredients: self-esteem, stress, the family history, and how family members get along.

Now let's sort through the details.

Solving the Mystery

When experts first began to describe those more likely to develop eating disorders, the picture looked this way: nice white girls from good homes. They did well in school, sports, and creative projects, but inside they didn't feel they measured up.

More and more experts now say that stereotype is wrong. Today kids of all different ethnic groups and backgrounds—rich, poor, urban, suburban, and rural—are known to have anorexia or bulimia.

No single profile describes everyone. But if you listen to the stories of girls with eating disorders you hear certain characteristics being repeated.

Perfect Little Girls

If we draw a profile of these characteristics, we find they describe girls trying to be what society considers perfect. They're sweet, cheerful, and get along with everybody. They have a shy smile when called on in class. They get their homework done on time and without any smudges.

They don't like to make waves. They don't want to talk back to their parents. In fact, they like being good and work hard at it. They've learned if they're quiet and well behaved, they get praised.

Then, as they near adolescence, the earth shifts beneath their feet. What that means and what happens next often depends on which expert is talking.

Some experts say that growing up scares young girls. They already have hints that life is going to be more violent and dangerous. Their parents can't always be there to protect them. As the pressure builds, so does their worrying.

Although they don't speak the words, although they aren't really aware of what they are doing, BLAM, something tells them that if they become skinny, they can keep their little-girl figures and their little-girl lives.

Parent Pleasers Rebel

Other experts believe these girls are not afraid to grow up. They're ready. They don't feel like kids anymore and don't want to be treated like kids.

But after spending all those years being perfect, they don't know how to rebel. How can they be bad when it's been so comfortable pleasing their parents? And, anyway, if they do start piercing their nose, wearing only black, and putting a lock on their door, that means they won't be living up to the family expectations. They're kind of anxious, too. There's always been an unspoken message from their mom and dad that without parental guidance they'll mess up.

These daughters are torn between wanting to make their parents happy—and pleasing themselves. They worry if they show their true feelings, they will upset their parents. Parents may even criticize their daughters—something these girls don't know how to handle.

They worry they might be rejected. Will that adult love be withdrawn? That's scary. The diet can be a backdoor way of confronting their parents.

Secret War of Independence

Still other experts say that anger has to be added to this mix. These girls understand the message. They understand they're supposed to be perfect: They're supposed to be polite and cheerful, and never be angry. If they are angry, they must hide it. If they show it, it might hurt someone.

But those rules are impossible to follow. So now these girls feel guilty for not being 100 percent cheerful. They start to lose control. How can they rein in their rebellious emotions? They don't know. They don't even know how to begin a conversation about all these conflicts raging inside them.

They've lost their way. Their whole worth is tied up in how others see them. Who they are is defined by their parents, their friends, the images on TV.

They feel overwhelmed by everything going on in their life. They have so many things to worry about, BLAM. To simplify it, they put all their panic in one place. They worry about their body.

Their body is what they can control, and with that as their focus, they are able to forget about their other problems. Their world tunnel-visions down to food. They can then begin to lose weight and feel prettier. That way they can be loved and their self-esteem will rise.

These perfect daughters will have declared their secret war of independence.

Perfect Parents

Who are the parents of at-risk girls? This is how therapists describe the families they see. They love their kids and show it. But they also pay close attention to work, the bills, and daily schedules. They worry about an increasingly troubled world.

Like the daughters they raise, lots of them are perfectionists.

These parents want their children to bring home good grades. They want them to eat right and be healthy. Mom and Dad also care about their own looks. They matter to them a lot, and to stay in shape they exercise. They probably are either on a diet or talking about one.

It's not unusual for girls with eating disorders to come from families where a sister, a first cousin, an aunt, or even a parent has had the same problem. Children do what parents do, not what parents say.

Anorexia: Rigid Rules

Experts use words like "highly functional" to describe the families of anorexics. This is where the supermoms live.

They're really into their kids and want to mold ideal daughters. To do that, they might even put a professional career on hold to focus on the family.

The fathers work hard and travel often. At home they may tune out. But some of them, along with the mothers, get so involved in their children's lives that the kids don't learn how to do things for themselves.

DOCTOR, PSYCHOLOGIST, NURSE, MINISTER

In one study, half of those with eating disorders had a parent working in a "caring" profession.[17]

These daughters become so attached to their parents they don't know how to make their own decisions. They just know they're supposed to obey and to succeed.

The parents seem either to control them too much with rigid rules or to leave them on their own too much. They think if their daughters have no complaints, they must be all right. They devote themselves to their other kids.

These families have trouble facing problems. Emotions aren't talked about or confronted. They bend over backward to avoid conflict.

Bulimic: Unpredictable Rules

The families of bulimics also think perfection and high achievement matter a lot, as does family loyalty. But life inside these homes isn't structured with rules and times and dates for everything. It's more unpredictable and disorganized.

When there are problems, people start feeling tense. Instead of dealing with problems, they ignore them. The only rule seems to be to keep in bad feelings. Instead, they bicker about incidental things.

Their daughters are expected to be together and rely on

themselves. They don't get as much hands-on care as anorexics. Still they and their moms are often close—too close. The mothers sometimes are possessive and distant at the same time. And even though they don't realize it, they have a hard time letting go of their daughters.

The dads sit behind the newspaper. When they are home in person, their minds may be out the door. They're warm, but they can't always be counted on to do things, like step in to deal with family trouble. These dads feel they knew how to spend time with their daughters as little girls. Once the girls hit adolescence, however, they become a mystery. They make their dads uncomfortable.

Three Keys to Solving the Mystery

Most, but not all, eating disorder experts are convinced that there are three other contributing factors to eating disorders. These are the problems we have trouble talking about. They are often family secrets.

Any one of these by itself increases the risk of family members turning to food as a way to control their lives. Any one of these means a predisposition, an inclination, to develop bulimia in particular, but also anorexia or even compulsive overeating.

The Shape of Moods

All families come with histories. These are the tales of the family's ups and downs through the years. They are also the collective information about family members' physical and mental well-being.

Maybe the mother in the family has emotions that change like the tides. Maybe the grandfather took his own life.

Maybe the father gets panic attacks when he crosses bridges.

These could add up to a family trait of emotional problems or what are known as mood and personality disorders. The disorders could range from depression to obsessive-compulsive behavior, where individuals repeat certain actions over and over.

The biological children in these families inherit their parents' genes. Genes determine not only the shape of their ears but also the shape of their emotions. If a biological parent experiences serious depression, it increases the children's chances of becoming seriously depressed, too. Their depression, though, might come out as an eating disorder.

Alcohol Blocks Out the World

Earlier in this chapter, some parents are described as perfectionists who value success. That's true. But there's another picture that must be painted, too.

Those with eating disorders may be growing up in homes where the adults turn to alcohol or drugs to regulate their moods and block out the world.

These children often lead stormy lives. They never know from one moment to the next what their day might be

CONTRIBUTING FACTORS

Your family history includes:
· mood disorders
· alcoholism/substance abuse
· verbal/physical/sexual abuse

like. They worry about inviting friends over. Will the adults in the house smell like beer and cigarettes? Will they be passed out on the couch? Will yesterday's dishes still be in the kitchen sink?

They learn early on that their parents are sending them

a chilling message. They can't depend on anybody but themselves. They are not allowed to need anything—from a tuna sandwich to a good-night hug. They certainly can't talk about their desire to be loved.

Food, these daughters discover, is something that can change their moods. Food is available. It's something over which they have some control, not like the rest of their life.

The Burden of Love

Some children live in homes where they are abused. They are yelled at, bullied, and routinely put down. They are never given credit. Maybe they hear they were an accident and not wanted.

Not surprisingly, these children feel unloved, as though they are a burden to the family. They feel that if they were not there, life for the others would be better. They decide to make their needs small and their body smaller, too.

They'll prove they can be self-sufficient. They can be unselfish, invisible. One way to do that is to stop eating.

Verbal abuse is hard to endure; physical violence causes grave harm. These children may show up at school with black eyes or slap marks on their faces, but usually the worst damage is hidden from others.

If they're ever questioned, they have been taught to say they got in a fight with—whomever. They learn not to talk, not to trust, not to feel.

The same is true with sexual abuse. The violence can be a one-time event where a girl sits on her uncle's lap and he puts his hand in an inappropriate place.

Or sexual abuse can be a frequent occurrence. The father, the stepfather, the mother's boyfriend, the mother in these families, comes into the child's bedroom and terrorizes the child—or children. They extract promises of secrecy. Most children don't have the ability to say they don't like what these adults are doing. They don't have the knowledge to withstand the threats.

In both physical and sexual abuse, some of these children teach themselves how to go numb to escape the emotional pain. Others use food to the same end. They find comfort in food. For them, for the moment, food is love. But then love turns to pain and guilt, and they reject it. They rid themselves of the food in their system.

chapter 10

food
for thought

Fear of Fat

You may know someone who is at risk of having a fear of
fat turn into a life-threatening eating disorder. You may be
afraid that you'll become that person. A few of you already
have. You may have recognized yourself on these pages.

Who's in Danger?

Two twelve-year-olds, Graciella and Lauren, could be in
danger of becoming eating-disorder statistics. Graciella
believes she saw where she was headed and stopped herself
before it was too late. Lauren doesn't even think she has a
problem. Here are their stories.

One Smart Bowling Ball

A couple months ago I went to the doctor. "You're a few
pounds overweight," he told me. "But don't worry. You're still
growing."

When I went home I wasn't thinking about it too much until my brother started teasing me, calling me a bowling ball. I went to sleep that night thinking about my weight and what I should do about it.

The next day I didn't have time for breakfast. At least that's what I told my mom. When I came home from school I was really hungry. My mom had the food ready because four o'clock is our dinnertime. I started to eat, but then I felt guilty.

My dad said, "What's wrong, Graciella?"

"Nothing," I said. "It just isn't a good day."

I excused myself for a minute and went to the kitchen. I drank three glasses of water and came back to the table. The water got me full, so I didn't eat that much more.

After dinner I went into the bathroom. I made myself throw up. I went to sleep feeling weird. But in the morning I felt good. I had lost two pounds.

The next day was Saturday. I woke up my lazy self at eleven o'clock. I wasn't really hungry, so I just had a glass of milk. I did my chores and watched some TV.

By the time dinner came, I was starving. I ate as much as I could. You know what I did next. I headed for the bathroom.

For a week I kept throwing up my dinner. I was surprised my parents hadn't noticed. I guess they thought I was in my bedroom instead of the bathroom. After those seven days I couldn't stand it anymore. It was too much of a hassle. It was disgusting . . . and stupid, too. If I had lost control, I could have died.

I'm proud of myself for stopping, but deep inside I'm mad for ever trying this way to lose weight. I may look like a bowling ball, but I'm a smart one.   —**Graciella, age twelve**

A Friend in Denial

People say to me, "Oh, Kim, I wish I had your body. You're so skinny." But to me, I look fat. Most of my friends weigh about 100 to 115. I weigh 92 pounds and that's over my ideal.

When I'm next to someone with 115-pound thighs, I see mine as bigger and fatter. People say to me, "Oh, you're perfect." I get good grades in school. I play all my favorite sports—soccer, basketball, and hockey. But still, all I ever want to be is thin.

One day my girlfriend Hannah starts asking a lot of questions. "Why do you let yourself get that skinny?" she wants to know. She's close to me like a sister so I tell her I know if I keep losing weight I'll be happier and my attitude will change so I won't be shy. I'll go farther in life and take more chances.

"I don't want to have you hurt or lose you," she says. "Is there a problem?"

"Not that I know of," I say. "I can't help it if you don't believe me." And you know what she answers?

"You're a friend in denial."   **—Kim, age twelve**

Dimensions of the Problem

How many of you are tempted to go on a diet? What's the dividing line between normal concern about weight and an eating disorder? By now you should have a clearer idea of the danger signs and symptoms. You should be able to look at the problem with more understanding.

Experts wonder how young people feel about dieting. They like to collect real numbers. They want to know the exact dimensions of a problem. They go to the source—you and your peers.

Different researchers hand out different self-tests, in which they ask students such questions as: Do you skip two or more meals a day? Do you feel disgusted with yourself, depressed, or very guilty after overeating?[19]

In Cincinnati, Ohio, 318 middle-income students in grades three through six answered questions about self-image, dieting, and bingeing. This is what they said: Thin is in. Forty-five percent of the students wanted to be thinner. Thirty-seven percent had already tried to lose weight. Ten percent had gone on eating binges.[20]

In another study researchers asked students: Do you want to lose weight now? Have you ever thought you looked fat to other people? Have you ever tried to lose weight by dieting?

They also had students circle the greatest amount of food they'd eaten in less than two hours (even if it wasn't exactly doughnuts, cookies, and ice cream) and how many times they'd done it. These are the quantities and frequencies listed.

QUANTITY
- less food than in the next example
- 2 doughnuts and a cup of ice cream and 2 cookies
- 4 doughnuts and a pint of ice cream and 5 cookies
- 6 doughnuts and a quart of ice cream and 10 cookies
- 8 doughnuts and a half-gallon of ice cream and 15 cookies

FREQUENCY
How many times in the last three months have you eaten lots of food in less than two hours?
- 1 or 2 times only
- 3 to 12 times

- 13 to 24 times
- 25 to 50 times
- more than 50 times

The students who answered these questions were in grades five through eight and lived in Charleston, South Carolina. Three thousand one hundred seventy-five completed self-tests with follow-up interviews. There were about equal numbers of girls and boys from many different backgrounds and both public and private schools. This is what they said.[21]

FAT ATTACK

55% of the girls wanted to lose weight now.
28% of the boys wanted to lose weight now.

54% of the girls felt they looked fat.
28% of the boys felt they looked fat.

43% of the girls had dieted.
20% of the boys had dieted.

6% of the girls had binged.
26% of the boys had binged.

The researchers were shocked.

These real numbers gave them information on which to base real conclusions. The numbers told them that more girls than boys don't like their bodies and are on diets right now. But boys also care about how they look. One out of five has tried to diet.

Girls begin dieting at younger ages, and they end up with eating disorders at younger ages than the experts thought. Looking around the room, the experts realized that students worried about being fat for no reason at all.

In their minds, students had an oversize body image that wasn't accurate.

What about You?

Below is a thirteen-question self-test. It's meant to help you recognize whether you are in trouble. Take out a piece of paper and check off the answers—Always, Sometimes, Never. Try to decide whether your attitude about food and your body is interfering with other parts of your life.

Think about what you look like and what you wish you looked like. Are they similar? Are they different? Do you think you are at risk of having an eating disorder?

Eating Attitude Quiz

Always   Sometimes   Never

I diet.

I eat diet food.

I feel fat and ask people,

   "Do you think I'm fat?"

I eat in secret or sneak food.

I eat only tiny portions.

I cut my food in small pieces.

I feel dizzy.

I exercise.

I like my stomach empty.

I am scared of being fat.

I have gone on eating binges

   where I feel I can't stop.

I throw up after I eat.

Other people think I'm too skinny.

Volunteers

One hundred eighth graders—twelve- and thirteen-year-olds—volunteered to take the self-test on food. Their answers follow. As you will see, 65 percent are scared of being fat. More than 50 percent diet. Nearly 30 percent binge, and 12 percent have thrown up after they eat.

These high numbers set off alarm bells. They meant that too many students could be headed for trouble. School counselors talked to the classes about self-esteem and self-image, nutrition and diets. They also met individually with girls and boys who recognized they were flirting with disaster.

Three students were referred to eating disorder counselors.

One Hundred Quiz Answers

1. I diet.	Always:	10
	Sometimes:	41
	Never:	47
2. I eat diet food.	Always:	6
	Sometimes:	50
	Never:	42
3. I feel fat and ask people, "Do you think I'm fat?"	Always:	20
	Sometimes:	31
	Never:	49
4. I eat in secret or sneak food.	Always:	4
	Sometimes:	30
	Never:	64
5. I eat only tiny portions.	Always:	4
	Sometimes:	54
	Never:	38

6. I cut my food in small pieces.	Always:	11
	Sometimes:	43
	Never:	42

7. I feel dizzy.	Always:	7
	Sometimes:	36
	Never:	54

8. I exercise.	Always:	51
	Sometimes:	43
	Never:	5

9. I like my stomach empty.	Always:	5
	Sometimes:	22
	Never:	72

10. I am scared of being fat.	Always:	24
	Sometimes:	41
	Never:	34

11. I have gone on eating binges where I feel I can't stop.	Always:	6
	Sometimes:	22
	Never:	71

12. I throw up after I eat.	Always:	2
	Sometimes:	10
	Never:	87

13. Other people think I'm too skinny.	Always:	17
	Sometimes:	32
	Never:	50

Too High a Price

What do your answers tell you about yourself? If most of them are in the **Never** column, you don't have much need for concern. Those in the **Sometimes** column are more revealing. You could be experimenting with potentially dangerous behavior.

And if most of your check marks are under **Always**, stop and evaluate what you are doing. If your diet is unsupervised, if it has lasted for several weeks, if you are developing eating rituals such as cutting your food into small pieces, if you binge eat, if you are making yourself throw up, if you feel dizzy—the price you are paying to lose weight is already too high.

You could have an eating disorder and should seek help.

chapter 11

help others,
help yourself

Winning and Losing

Those with eating disorders become experts on how to eat.
They don't want to talk about what's really bothering them.
They just want to talk about food.

It's a safe topic, and the other stuff isn't.

If this way of thinking has lasted more than a few
weeks, they're in trouble. The longer they act like this, the
harder it is to change. It's their drug. They always get some
kind of rush, some positive feeling, even if it's only for five
minutes.

They feel relief by not eating. It's a contest they've won.
They like how their stomach feels against their backbone.
They escape bad feelings by munching away on Reese's
Pieces. They are triumphant when they throw up. They've
beaten the system.

Overcoming this mental food fight takes more than just

changing how they eat. Eating disorders are mind-body problems. To change the way they eat, they have to change what's bothering them. They have to realize that the anorexia, the bulimia, is their enemy. It can kill them. They have to stop their eating patterns and replace them with healthier patterns.

It isn't easy. They could be battling for their life.

Trying to Help

Three girls—Josette, age eleven, Noelle, age twelve, and Anne, age twelve—each know someone with an eating disorder. They offered to talk about what happened when they tried to be a helping friend.

This is what Josette has to say.

Shadow Man's Daughter

Heather, my best friend in the whole world, goes back and forth between anorexia and bulimia. This has devastated me. I love her and would never want anything to happen to her.

Three of us decided we had to tell our school nurse. The nurse notified her parents what to watch for. They did. Heather ended up with almost every symptom. We finally got her to admit to herself that she had this disease and she needed help.

She did a lot of research and began to get back to her normal self. Everyone thought she'd recovered. Everyone, that is, except me.

"What's really going on?" I asked her.

"Just some personal stuff," she said.

I pushed her. I mean, we are best friends.

"It's my parents," she said. "My mom calls Dad the Shadow Man. He's never home. She thinks he's running around. She says she doesn't have enough money to get a divorce. I'm totally upset and just can't eat."

I didn't know what to say to help her. I always thought they were the perfect family. A few weeks later I noticed she was losing weight again. One night I ate over at her house. We finished dinner and she said, "I have to use the bathroom."

I went to the door and listened. I could tell what she was doing. When I got home, I asked my mom for advice. She said, "Don't do anything unless you're positive."

"But I am." I'm still waiting for my mom's answer.

—**Josette, age eleven**

You're Gonna Die

One day in the cafeteria I noticed that Amanda, one of my friends, was looking upset. I went up to her and asked, "Hey, what's wrong?"

"I'm sick," she said, and the look on her face told me it was something more serious than a cold. "The guidance counselor thinks I have anorexia. It's not true. Remember I had mono last year."

I didn't believe her. Since the year before, she had lost thirty pounds. She was five feet five and weighed only about ninety-five. Still she was forever complaining that she was too fat. She would cook lots of carrot cakes and zucchini breads, but I never saw her eat them. She would just sit there, rubbing her wrist and her elbow. Strange, huh?

Amanda wanted to keep this thing secret, but news spread. Some students started crying. But other students yelled at her. "You're gonna die." I couldn't let myself believe that. Pity wouldn't help the situation. Neither would sympathy. It would only make her more upset and probably confuse her. But I had to do something.

I wanted to help her live, not wait for her to die. I tried to make her eat. I tried to convince her she wasn't fat. She waved me away. I finally realized only she could make the difference. She had to help herself.

—**Noelle, age twelve**

The Pencil versus the Football

My cousin, I'd rather not say her name, has a problem. She's skinny as a pencil, but she thinks she's fat as a football. What she's doing isn't normal.

At breakfast she eats like a pig and then goes into the bathroom. Fifteen minutes later she comes out all smiles. At lunch she always lies and says she bought lunch or ate at someone's house. Then at dinner she just eats a little.

Later, before she goes to sleep, she goes to the bathroom for over a half hour, and she's not just brushing her teeth.

She's always exercising, too, so when people notice she's getting skinnier, they think that's the reason. They don't know what I know.

Finally I told my parents and her parents, but they didn't believe me. I got so upset that I even told the guidance counselor. That was a good move because guidance called some people connected with an eating disorder program.

My cousin agreed to go, and I think it's helping her. She's

opening up to me again and telling me what happened. She says she's much happier with herself now. I'm glad I got involved. **—Anne, age twelve**

Breaking the Silence

Do you think you know someone with an eating disorder? If you're worried, here are some suggestions about breaking the silence.

First, pick a time when you're both relaxed and just hanging out. Talk about how you feel, not what you think she should or shouldn't be doing.

How do you get the conversation started? You could tell her you're concerned. Is she worried about something? Lately, she always seems upset. What's going on?

You *don't* want to talk about her eating behavior. You just want to let her know that her worry has been noticed. You are a worried friend.

Your friend may not want to have this conversation. She may tell you there's nothing wrong with her. She may even get mad at you.

Even if she listens to you, it doesn't mean she's hearing what you're saying. It doesn't mean anything will change. The only behavior you can change is your own. You can talk to her. You can talk to her parents, your parents, your teachers, your preachers, your school counselors. But only when your friend *wants* to change can anyone really help her.

Facing Facts

Have you been finding yourself on these pages? Have the descriptions of people with eating disorders sounded like you? If the answer is yes, you've taken a big first step. You've just let yourself know that you have a problem.

The next step is to figure out what you can and can't do to change.

What you can change is your ability to separate fact from fantasy. It's important not just to know the difference but also to act on what you know. When you watch TV, for instance, repeat to yourself this kind of conversation: Why are all those women so skinny? Would it really matter if the characters they play weighed more? Would it change what happens in any important way?

When you go to the mall, when you walk down the school hall, look around. Do you see many people who actually look like the models and stars? Are they what you see in your everyday life?

DON'TS AND DO'S WHEN HELPING A FRIEND

Don't say she's killing herself.

Don't play food cop and tell her what to eat.

Don't even talk about food, calories, or eating habits.

Don't try to be her therapist.

Don't push her to tell you more than she wants.

Don't think it's your job to solve this problem.

Do say you want to help.

Do talk about your problems along with hers.

Do give her information, this book, and maybe a suggested place to go for help.

Do listen without judging her.

Do remind her there are more benefits to recovering than there are from the disorder.

Do ask for adults' help.

Ask yourself, Why is it that most programs with overweight people usually have them on the receiving end of jokes? We're taught not to make fun of people with disabilities. We're taught not to make fun of older people. Why is it okay to make fun of people who are heavy?

Look at ads with skinny women. Ask yourself, Who decided that skinny is the only kind of beauty?

The Puzzle

You admit to yourself that you have problems. You might not be able to identify them right away, but you can start to put together the pieces of the puzzle. You want to close the gap between you and yourself. What does that mean? Starving yourself, stuffing yourself, and purging are all ways of distancing you from yourself and your real feelings. These are ways in which you stop learning how to love yourself.

Now it's time for you to start changing that process.

FIVE THINGS YOU CAN'T CHANGE

1. The thin-is-beautiful message going out across the nation.
2. The diets of high-fashion models, Hollywood superstars, ballet dancers, and figure skaters.
3. The genes you've inherited from your biological parents.
4. The height and basic build of your body.
5. Yesterday.

Figuring It Out

• Start to ask yourself: If I weren't upset about food today, what would be on my mind? If I weren't upset about the calories, would I be able to enjoy the Fourth of July picnic? If I weren't thinking about gaining weight, would I be able to go out with my friends?

• Start to teach yourself to understand your true feelings. You don't want to keep creating physical pain—the gnawing hunger—to hide from the emotional pain brought on by the hidden problems. You don't want to keep eating and throwing up. Once you've thrown up, you're exhausted, and the underlying problems remain unchanged.

• Start to allow yourself to grow up. It's okay to worry, and it's okay to talk about problems. If your parents handle problems by avoiding them, talk to them about it. Tell them you have things that bother you, and you need to face them. You no longer want them shoved under the rug. Regardless of whether your fears are more about tomorrow or today, remind yourself and your parents that you can get through them.

• Start to gain control over your life. You don't want food running the show. You want to teach yourself how to deal with your emotions in a healthy way. When you're feeling blue, angry, or ready to explode, sit down and try to figure out why. Then work on real change, not losing yourself in a food binge, a calorie chart, or an exercise routine.

• Start to take time each day to practice some stress-reduction technique, meditate, or sit quietly and focus on your favorite place to relax.

• Start to learn how to accept compliments. When your parents say, "You're a beautiful girl," don't think, "I'm their daughter. That's what they have to say." Instead say, "Thanks," and give them a hug. When your friends say, "You have a great figure," don't say, "You're out of your mind. I'm a sausage." Say, "Thanks." Other people often have a better idea of what you look like than you do. Listen to them.

Changing the Message

• Stop feeling it's wrong to have a good time. Make sure that each day you make room for fun. Do something goofy. Do something silly. Do something that puts a smile on your face. Fun helps you get rid of tension and chases a bad mood away. If you can't remember when you last really laughed, that alone says something is wrong.

TALKING BACK

Stand in front of a full-length mirror and talk to yourself. So it sounds crazy. Try it anyway. That mirror has been picking on you for too long. You haven't been able to stay away from it. But most of what it tells you is lousy.

Face it. You've been using the mirror to discipline yourself.

It's time to talk back. Now you tell yourself that you'd love banana cream pie, but you can't eat it every day. You don't want to gain that much weight. Starting today, you are changing. Starting today, challenge your old attitude about food. Starting today, say to yourself, Once in a while it's okay to have a slice of pie. Other people do that and they're not overweight.

• Stop hiding from the world. Spend time each day with your family, your friends, or in some activity that makes you feel good. Think about volunteering to help at a day care center, doing errands for senior citizens, or tutoring a younger student. Then remind yourself you are a fabulous person. You should be proud of yourself for how you contribute.

• Stop letting yourself get so hungry that you think about bingeing. Instead, each day have some healthy food that you really like. If you don't feel you're forcing yourself to go hungry, you won't need to binge on your secret favorite food.

• Stop stepping on the scale every chance you have. Stop

dressing in the dark. Stop hiding your body in baggy layers of clothes. Stop being afraid to experiment with clothes that might make you feel confident. Stop checking your reflection in passing windows. Stop worrying about what people think of you.

• Stop being at war with your body. Pamper it. Take soothing bubble baths and gentle showers. Massage your feet and hands. Paint your nails. Do stretches and relaxation exercises.

• Stop putting yourself down at every opportunity. Eating disorders are not about food as much as being unable to see your body the way it is. You develop a negative self-image because you send yourself lousy messages about how you look.

• Change those messages. Write in a journal. On one page write all the things going on in your head that say you're no good. On the other page argue against those beliefs. Write all the positive things about yourself and your life. Keep doing this until there are more things on the positive page than the negative page.

• Write in a journal how you feel during a binge or the high you get from fasting. List all the ways the disorder has changed your life. Make another list of different ways you can fight the urge to binge or starve. Realize that an eating disorder is the enemy. You can't get well unless you make a decision to fight it.

Make a third list of the lies this disorder tells you. You

think it's your friend? Then why is your hair falling out? Why do you always have a sore throat from throwing up? Why are you so tired? Life is about choices and you can choose to get better.

Revenge of Chicken Legs

Keep talking. This time practice complimenting yourself. Did someone call you Chicken Legs? So what, he's just stupid. Your revenge is not worrying about it. Everybody has good and bad characteristics. Give yourself a break, and say nothing but kind things to yourself, starting with what great eyes you have, what long, graceful fingers.

Go back and study your mirror reflection. Start to see the real you, not just what you think others see. Keep doing this until you no longer get upset. Then relax and focus on your real talents.

Look at yourself as a whole person. Look at what you have to offer others. You are the sum total of all your characteristics. Stand there and think about your brains, your ability in math, your thoughtfulness toward others. Your motivation and your personality have much more value than what you weigh.

What matters is not the wrapping but what's inside the package.

chapter 12

couch potatoes vs. sweet potatoes

Couch Potatoes

Some people can eat anything, have an all-around yucky diet, and never gain an ounce. Other people look at a grape and get fatter. There is a range of what is normal. And especially around the ages of ten and eleven, it's just about normal to be somewhat pudgy. Within another year or so the body starts to thin out. The weight and the height come into balance.

But this is not always the case, and here's where things get tricky and dangerous, too. The national couch potato population is way up. Fifteen years ago one person in four was overweight. Now it's one person in three.[22] An ever-growing number of people are ever growing.

FOOD ON THE RUN

More than a third of all the restaurants in America serve fast food. Each day they feed a hundred million people.[23]

Family Trees, Taco Bells, and Twizzlers

Why are more people overweight? For some there are genetic reasons, a family tree with parents and other close relatives, all heavy. But other issues come into play.

Even though it sounds strange, people your age are encouraged not to eat right. You've got your daily dose of ads telling you to come on down—to Wendy's, Pizza Hut, Taco Bell. They're nearby, fun, and the food tastes yummy. These ads don't mention that most items on the menu are also really fattening.

WHITE, WHEAT, OR RYE?

The five favorite sandwiches that kids take to school, in order of preference:

1. peanut butter and jelly
2. ham
3. bologna
4. cheese
5. turkey [24]

Life's so busy today, there's not always enough time to home-cook a meal. That means your parents may even lead the way to pick up dinner at some local restaurant. The portions are big. The food is predictable. A bucket of Kentucky Fried Chicken bought anywhere in the world tastes the same.

That's more than can be said for, say, a honeydew melon. You pay a dollar fifty, slice it up, and what? It's tough to guess a sweet one from one with no flavor. Maybe it's even gone bad. And now you're out the money.

You head for the fast-food line. All your friends seem to be there. And now fast-food restaurants have moved into thousands of school cafeterias. You can have your favorite McDonald's right there. So you go for the fries and the tater tots over the carrots and celery. Now all you need is for them to sell Twizzlers.

A body needs eight to ten glasses of water a day. There's hardly a decent water fountain to be found. You settle for a soda and a candy bar for sale as class fund-raisers.

School and community gyms and sports programs are reduced because of budget cuts. And your mother says you have to come straight home after classes, anyway. She doesn't want you out running around getting into trouble.

You sit in front of the TV, eating. The only thing you're exercising is your mouth.

Hold the Fries, Pass the Sweet Potatoes

- Switch from high-sugar breakfast cereal to low-sugar cereal
- Switch from whole milk to 1 percent, 2 percent, or skim milk
- Switch from soda to fruit juice
- Switch from eggs to egg substitutes
- Switch from white bread to whole-grain bread or pita
- Switch from salt as a seasoner to herbs and lemon juice
- Switch from fried chicken to skinless, broiled chicken
- Switch from hamburgers to veggie burgers, sunburgers, or turkey burgers

Deadly Lesson

Doctors are worried. They're trying to teach people a vital lesson. More than half the leading causes of death are related to the food we eat. And these diseases begin to develop in the teen years and even younger.

Being overweight is hazardous to your health, these doctors say. Obesity can kill. Go on a diet. Eat healthy. Lose weight, they say. That kind of advice is given while forgetting that dieting can come with its own set of problems. As you've learned, dieting can turn deadly.

So what are you supposed to do?

First, relax. There's nothing wrong with dieting if you're doing it the right way and for the right reasons. There's nothing wrong with dieting if you are too heavy and have a supervised plan. You have to let the adults in your life know what you want to do and why.

You should talk to them about what food you might want—or not want—in order to help you drop some pounds. Weight loss should be gradual. The first few pounds come off fairly quickly. After that, though, the process slows down.

· Switch from french fries to sweet potatoes, baked potatoes, or baked chips
· Switch from regular pizza to pizza without cheese
· Switch from just any vegetable to carrots, spinach, collard greens, and red peppers
· Switch from just any fruit to papaya, cantaloupe, strawberries, and oranges
· Switch from Dunkaroos, Kit Kats, and Neon Bandits to rice cakes, raisins, and dried apple slices.[25]

HAPPY EATING!

Dieting requires eating certain foods in moderation. More important, it requires patience.

Bathing Suit Weather

But here's the danger. You've had a "BLAM moment" and made an instant decision. You want to lose weight *now*. You go off on your own, without much thought and with no real plan. You decide to diet without knowing exactly what you should and shouldn't eat.

Instead your tendency is to shut down. You try to skip whole meals, not just cut back. A skipped meal—even if it's breakfast—isn't the end of the world. But when an empty stomach makes you cranky and inattentive, that should teach you a fast lesson.

Healthy food, not a Yodel and a soda on the run, is what you need to be able to focus. Many of you aren't sure which foods are essential and which you can eliminate.

You know that adults always seem to be pushing vegetables. Did you know, however, that some vegetables—carrots and spinach, for example—are better for you than others? Even some fruits are better than others, and some breads, too. The same is true for milk, meat, and cereal.

But you don't want to bother with the details. What worries you is that bathing suit weather is four weeks away.

Hold the Dunkaroos

A healthy diet should be a natural part of your life. It shouldn't come with rigid rules and restrictions that mess with your head.

If, today, you want to improve your diet—and probably lose extra weight—here are some food switches you can make.

Eighty-six Guinea Pigs

You've just read nutritional advice, a responsible way to start to improve your diet. But what do real girls and boys your age eat?

Eighty-six middle school students agreed to be guinea pigs. Each day for a week they wrote down what they ate and drank. They were sophisticated, smart kids who knew about calories, fat content, and the difference between ravioli and manicotti.

But here's their reality.

Nearly all of them had at least one meal home alone in that seven-day period. Sixty-four of them skipped at least one meal, and most skipped more than one, often breakfast.

Of the students who never missed a chance to eat, what they put in their mouth varied. One twelve-year-old's first-day menu read like this:

BURP

breakfast:	slice of fat-free chocolate chip cake, glass of apple juice
snack:	two Twizzlers
lunch:	cookie and water
snack:	two Brontosauruses
dinner:	hot dog on a bun, brussels sprouts, baked beans, soda

Now compare it to this girl's one day of meals.

FAT ATTACK

breakfast:	waffle with syrup and butter, orange juice
lunch:	sandwich with cold cuts, soda
dinner:	pork chops, apple sauce, tater tots, ketchup, zucchini, soda
snack:	Milky Way, potato chips, and a Devil Dog

Another student ate the same lunch every day for a week: a turkey-and-cheese sandwich, fries, and chocolate milk.

Still another loved snacks: cookies, bagel dogs, Goldfish crackers, Cheez Doodles, potato chips, doughnuts, and M&M's. He washed these down with milk, water, Coke, orange soda, cream soda, root beer, Pepsi, or juice. He recorded what time he ate, too: 7:40 A.M., 1:05 P.M., 3 P.M., 7:30 P.M., 9 P.M.

Here are the complete records from three more students.

Weekly Food Log 1

3\14
  Breakfast: toast, orange juice — 7:20
  Lunch: cookie, lemonade — 1:30
  Snack: gum — 2:50
  Dinner: peas, yoo-hoo — 6:20
3\15
  Breakfast: yoo-hoo, bagel — 7:10
  Lunch: cookie, iced tea — 1:30
  Snack: lollipop — 2:55
  Dinner: turkey burger, Gatorade — 5:20
3\16
  Breakfast: bagel — 6:50
  Lunch: cookie, iced tea — 1:30
  Snack: lollipop — 3:05
  Dinner: turkey sandwich, coke — 6:00

3\17
   Breakfast: Toast, Orange juice - 7:00
   Lunch: Cookie, iced tea - 1:32
   Dinner: Sweet Potato - 6:20
3\18
   Breakfast: cereal - 9:00
   Lunch: NONE
   Dinner: Pizza, tater tots - 9:00
3\19
   Breakfast: cereal - 8:30
   Lunch: grilled cheese - 1:50
   Dinner: turkey burger - 6:00

3\20
   Breakfast: toast, Orange juice - 7:00
   Lunch: iced tea - 1:25
   Snack: gum - 2:45
   Dinner: mashed Potatoes - 5:30

Weekly Food Log 2

3/14
   Breakfast: gum
   Lunch: —
   Dinner: 1/2 of a hamburger
3/15
   Breakfast: —
   Lunch: Fries
   Dinner: 2 slices of bread

3/16
   Breakfast: —
   Lunch: gum
   Dinner 1/2 slice of pizza

3/17
   Breakfast: 1/2 a bowl of cereal
   Lunch: —
   Dinner: —

3/18
   Breakfast: gum
   Lunch: gum
   Dinner: —

3/19
   Breakfast: —
   Lunch: —
   Dinner: soup

Weekly Food Log 3

3/14

Breakfast: Life cereal, skim milk

Lunch: BLT sandwich,
french fries, 2% milk,
grape Airhead

Dinner: homemade Chinese
food, rice, glass of skim
milk

Snacks: some cotton candy,
buttered roll, 3 glasses of
cranberry juice, 2 glasses
of water

3/15

Breakfast: Life cereal, skim
milk, orange, banana

Lunch: BLT sandwich, french
fries, 2% milk, 1/2 orange

Dinner: pizza (1 slice), Sprite

Snack: 1 "trial size" pound cake,
2 glasses of water

3/16
Breakfast: toasted bagel,
glass of water
Lunch: ham-bologna-salami-
cheese sandwich, 1 coffee
cake, Sunny Delight, Jell-O
in a cup, 1/2 orange
Dinner: homemade Chinese
food, Wendy's junior burger,
large fries, bottle of
cranberry juice
3/18
Breakfast: nothing
Lunch: hot dog, banana, Life
cereal, skim milk
Dinner: corned beef, mashed
potatoes, carrots skim
milk, french crumb cake
3/19
Breakfast: Life cereal, skim
milk

Lunch: pickle, ham-and-roast beef sandwich
Dinner: pizza (2 slices), Sprite
Snack: iced tea, frozen yogurt (vanilla), candy

3/20
Breakfast: Life cereal, skim milk, orange juice, banana
Lunch: Arby's chicken filet sandwich with curly fries and regular fries, iced tea
Dinner: fish sticks, spaghetti, skim milk

Snack: apple, candy, 4 Samoa Girl Scout cookies, glass of Gatorade

Horrified Nutritionists

Several nutritionists looked over the lists and offered their thoughts. They said that when adults are asked to record their meals, they often cheat, leaving out things so it looks like they eat better and less.

The nutritionists felt the students were honest. They were horrified by what a lot of them were eating . . . but not surprised.

"Is the first girl a sort-of vegetarian?" they wondered. She ate no red meat; she did, however, eat poultry—the turkey burgers and sandwich. She never drank milk. The nutritionists hoped that at best she might be allergic to it.

Gum isn't food, and lunch should be more nutritious than a cookie and lemonade. They worried, too, that the only fruit she had was in the form of juice. Better than nothing, but they wished she had a whole something—grapes, strawberries, papaya.

The second student they worried about the most. She ate next to nothing. She could have been sick that week, or they were looking at the diet of an anorexic.

The third student had the best variety in what she ate. They thought what she had for breakfast, in general, was fine, and at least on two days she included fresh fruit. They also said that for a twelve-year-old having low-fat or skim milk was a good idea. Plus, she was the only one of the students to have fish, even though it was fish sticks.

Then they came to the ham-bologna-salami-cheese sandwich followed by a coffee cake. It stopped them cold. She's undoing the good she started in the morning. There's too much fat, along with fried foods and sweets.

***

Balancing on the Pyramid

What should these students—and you—be eating to lead healthy, long lives? Take a look at the Food Pyramid on page 93. If you have any religious or dietary restrictions, leave those foods off your list. After that, the wider the sections, the more those foods should be included in your diet.

The best diets are built on a foundation of grains: cereal, bread, rice, and pasta. The next level is made up of foods from plants, fruits, and vegetables. After that in smaller and smaller portions come foods mainly from animals. You should have some, but not much milk, yogurt, and cheese; meat, poultry, fish, beans, eggs, and nuts.

What should make the fewest appearances on your menu may be some of your all-time favorites: salad dressings, olive oil, and butter, as well as the sweets, the treats, and the sodas.

How to Start Making Changes

Human bodies are amazing things which, when given half a chance, will tell you, their owners, when and what to eat. The owners' job is to listen. In other words, at first let body hunger be the guide, and the body will tell you when it's time for food.

Don't be concerned about limiting your choices. Experiment. Don't just automatically think that certain foods are nasty. Don't judge yourself. You should just eat. Your goal is to learn—or relearn—how to eat without dieting or bingeing. In fact, starving a body is a major cause of out-of-control eating. And the food you binge on is the same food you spend the rest of your time trying to avoid.

Next, start to think about eating the right things. You

shouldn't focus on gaining or losing weight as much as eating the right combination of the right foods. Try to avoid all that plastic food the fast-food industry keeps putting in front of you. And cut back on the food that's been in the freezer for a year. Instead, try to include more fresh food in your diet.

After a while, as you get used to eating without fear, you'll find your own natural body weight. It might not be the model-perfect size, but you'll be happier. And once you relax a little about what you eat, you'll start making food choices based on what will help you lead a longer, healthier life.

Diet Right

My mom says, "It's not healthy to go on diets when you're young, but it's okay to watch what you eat." That's what I'm trying to do because I'm heavier than a lot of my friends. I'm having smaller portions, and I'm still not depriving myself of anything. If I do that, I'll want to eat even more.

I have learned that I must have self-confidence to lose weight. I must set reasonable goals. When I achieve those goals I am proud of myself and go further, but not over the limit my mom and I have agreed on.

I know, too, that I don't have to go on crazy diets or have some eating disorder to better my appearance. I just have to get a balanced diet and good nutrition and exercise regularly. This way I'm not hurting myself mentally, emotionally, or physically. And I'll feel good about myself in the end!

—Madelyn, age thirteen

The Food Guide Pyramid

A Guide to Daily Food Choices

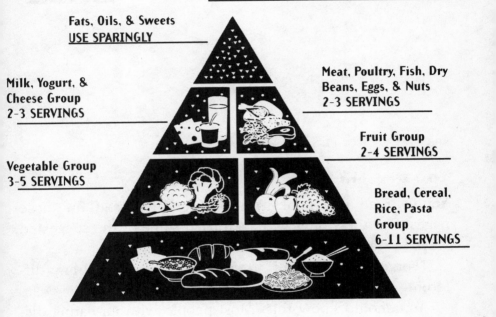

KEY
◻ Fat (naturally occurring and added)
▼ Sugars (added)

These symbols show fat and added sugars in foods.

Fats, Oils, & Sweets
USE SPARINGLY

**Milk, Yogurt, &
Cheese Group
2-3 SERVINGS**

**Meat, Poultry, Fish, Dry
Beans, Eggs, & Nuts
2-3 SERVINGS**

**Fruit Group
2-4 SERVINGS**

**Vegetable Group
3-5 SERVINGS**

**Bread, Cereal,
Rice, Pasta
Group
6-11 SERVINGS**

WHAT IS THE FOOD GUIDE PYRAMID?

The Pyramid is an outline of what to eat each day. It's not a rigid pre-scription, but a general guide that lets you choose a healthful diet that's right for you.

The Pyramid calls for eating a variety of foods to get the nutrients you need and at the same time the right amount of calories to maintain a healthy weight.

The Pyramid also focuses on fat because most American diets are too high in fat, especially saturated fat.

soar

100 Percent Sure

You've read this book. You've found yourself on these pages. For a few days you even tried some of the suggested ways to start changing and healing.

"Forget it," you think to yourself. "I don't feel any different."

You should know this: Most people with an eating disorder are never 100 percent sure they want to give it up. It's not an easy battle, and their desire to get better varies from day to day.

But maybe right now is the time to reach out for help. Maybe right now you should go find the most important adult in your life, the one you feel most comfortable with, and say you need help solving this problem.

When you're ready for help, don't worry, treatment is

there. What this means to you in particular depends on how strong you are emotionally and physically.

You could try therapy, sorting out your feeling with the help of a person trained in dealing with eating disorders, joining a group with other people confronting the same issues, or attending family therapy sessions along with one or both parents.

You could go with a variation of what you've been doing. Instead of centering your attention on food and strenuous exercise, learn meditation or relaxation techniques, such as yoga or tai chi chuan.

Instead of being at war with your body, work to find comfort from it. Schedule a series of appointments with a massage therapist or osteopath, a doctor who treats medical problems with body manipulation.

If your life is in danger, a parent may take any decision away from you. This is tricky because that's been part of your original problem. Still, you have to save your life before you can repair it.

You may have to be hospitalized temporarily. The staff in most places is made up of doctors, therapists, nutritionists, nurses, and teachers. They will all work with you to begin to put the pieces of your life together.

In the end, however, you're the one who has to be willing to meet them halfway. You have to take those beginning steps in order to bring about change.

Adjust Your Passion

It's time to begin your journey. You know how long it took to get yourself to where you are today. It will take that much time and longer to plot this new course. The path of recovery is a difficult one to follow. If you relapse, ask yourself, "Why am I returning to those eating behaviors? Why now? What must I do so I don't need them?"

Then as you progress, remind yourself that you are a person of amazing dedication and determination. You have been making a heroic, if misguided, effort to change your size and shape.

You have been using superhuman power to control your weight. Now take that strength and energy, and use it in a positive way. First, work to benefit yourself; next, work to benefit the world around you.

Don't give up your passion. Simply adjust its direction. You will soar.

United Voids

If given the chance to change any one of my features, I wouldn't go through with it. I am what I am, inside and out. I may not be anywhere near beautiful, but even so, all my body parts and facial details are a part of ME.

Whether it's my numerous scars and bruises or even my rare webbed toes, everything is just another puzzle piece into your heart.

What if, say, we all suddenly were blessed with eternal beauty? Imagine every one of us standing tall with sparkling bright eyes; rich, shiny hair; and skinny, sexy bodies. Let's face it: We'd all become a race of united voids, empty and lacking our own individual outlooks.

Boring.

—Sadie, age twelve

✳ ✳ ✳

Parts Two and Three

Part two of this book speaks to your parents. You're welcome to read it or skip it and go on to part three. There you'll find a list of addresses and phone numbers of organizations involved with the issues of eating disorders, healthy eating, and children's well-being. There is also a list of other books on this and related topics, as well as information about the student and adult experts whose words you've been seeing on these pages.

For Adult Readers

chapter 14

food
fight

Our Puppets

As parents, we love our kids. We struggle to do the right thing in raising them. We read the books, compare notes with family and friends, and pray for a little luck.

Then those sweet children of ours turn eleven and twelve. Physically girls start coming up with a few curves—and acne. Preteens feel they'll die of embarrassment. But other changes are beginning to take place, ones that are far more alarming to them and to us. They are the changes over which we have little control: the pressures from society, TV, music, movies, and their peers.

Our youngsters are knocking on the door of adolescence, a different world from the one we entered at their age. It's meaner, more violent, more sexual, and less forgiving. Our sons have to make certain changes to adapt, but our daughters are the ones who have to alter their psyches.

Since they were old enough to handle the remote, they've been channel surfing through programs in which women are routinely raped, terrorized, and beaten. Yes, women are now allowed to play the roles of doctors and lawyers, but they still better not be ugly. They still have to have great bodies.

Our daughters have been learning about sex since an equally young age, if not on the afternoon soap operas, then on the ever-present MTV music videos. We might have been warned about sex and unplanned pregnancies. They hear about sex and death; AIDS is part of their vocabulary.

Home is no longer the safe haven it used to be. They know their parents can't protect them once they're out of view. And more often than not, they don't want us to. Only the unpopular kids stay close to their parents.

We're busily encouraging them to keep up with their wide-ranging interests, keep participating in sports, sign up to create a science project, and certainly not to start fretting about dates. We want them to remain true to themselves. But they sometimes feel as if they're our puppets and have to jump when we pull the strings.

"Who am I?" they wonder. And they worry, too. Sometimes they worry because they're sensitive kids and feel insecure. Sometimes they worry in proportion to the increase in personal and family problems—a best friend's abandonment, a switch to a large middle school, their parents' divorce. That's a lot to handle, especially at this vulnerable age, and it may well throw them off balance. It's a difficult time for everybody.

Many of them begin to evolve into sadder and angrier people. They begin to shut down. They take their bright stars and hide them under a barrel.

Now add to this brew our national obsession with thinness. It is the defining standard of beauty for much of society. There is almost no way a parent can fight it. We may well buy into it, too. Our daughters carry this obsession a step further, though. They want to be popular and have come to believe that looks are what it's about. They have just got to be attractive.

A Daughter's Cry

Sometimes I wish I could have made myself. I mean my inside is great (in my opinion), but the outside, who knows. I'm not that overweight, but I'm leaning toward that way. When I go clothes shopping, I spend too much time trying to find an outfit where I won't look like a hippo. I don't want to be teased anymore.

Last month I went to a family reunion. In a wink of an eye, everyone

A Trigger

Our children already stand in the line of fire. And the combination of youth, stress, and self-doubt can turn potentially lethal with the pull of an emotional trigger. It could be as fleeting as a brother's casual comments about weight made in front of friends or a teacher's assignment of two hours' homework on the first day of soccer practice.

It could be as significant as an overheard conversation in which a dad broods about the next round of layoffs at work. The mother fears with her husband they may soon be dangling at the end of a financial rope.

Some kids panic and lose control. They develop migraines, allergies, rashes. They might self-mutilate, refuse to go to school, or generally make us crazy. Or they might return again and again to what they think is reflected in the mirror. They don't see reality. They see a meatball with a nose they hate and Fred Flintstone feet.

They make a decision to take control over what is within their reach: food. They diet. At first this seems both benign and positive. It can be such a quiet—or secret—decision that we don't even notice. If we do, initially, we probably join the chorus of praise. Our society's habit is to encourage those who try to lose weight.

> started talking about how I looked. I couldn't keep listening. I went to the bathroom and started to throw up for about fifteen minutes without stopping. My mom came in and made one of her speeches. She said what mattered was how I look at myself, not how others look at me. I don't know if I think she's right, but at least it got me thinking and not hurting so much.
>
> **—Polly, age ten**

Of course, the vast majority of people losing and gaining that same few pounds escapes without their efforts turning into an eating disorder. Why should our children be any different? But as we know, a certain percentage of youngsters, mainly younger and younger females, lose themselves in the process.

Sorting through confusing emotions takes skill. And the truth is, most of us aren't always good at that. Kids have even less practice. So they go for the easy answer. Anyway, they think they've stumbled on a magic power. If losing five pounds is good, losing ten pounds will be better. If ten is better, what about fifteen?

They take a fateful next step on this dangerous journey. Losing weight becomes a common goal shared with their peers. Some of them, however, begin to concentrate solely on their shape.

Some start to starve themselves and call it a diet. Others secretly binge. They escape into food, stuffing themselves uncontrollably. Then, filled with shame, they purge. They work to eliminate all food from their body.

Regardless of what specific food rituals each individual comes up with, these youngsters share certain characteristics. They have an extreme fear of being fat and a distorted body image. Their sense of self is equally distorted: they feel extremely inadequate. They also are not concerned that their eating patterns could have dangerous medical consequences.

They are overwhelmed by trying to make sense of all the messages society keeps throwing them. Their actions are just their best attempts to bring order to what they have come to view as chaos.

Horror Stories

Experts on eating disorders all have horror stories. They can tell us about the twenty-year-old who weighed sixty-two pounds when she finally showed up at a psychiatrist's office. "It was as if her brain were broken," was how she was described.

They can tell us about the sixteen-year-old stay-at-home kid who narrowed his diet to egg whites, cottage cheese, and pears. He then became a fanatic about his exercise routine: weights, sit-ups, and cross-country running—rain, snow, or sunshine.

And they can tell us about the eighteen-year-old who could have weighed a slim enough 110 pounds but actually weighed only seventy-three.

Her parents were desperate. They did what desperate parents often do. They checked their daughter into a hospital for treatment. She couldn't believe it. She was furious at them. She was fine, just fine, she told them.

In the hospital she had a structured day, starting with a weigh-in first thing in the morning. The scale, though, was turned backward so she couldn't see the figure.

She met the ten other girls in this particular inpatient facility. They eyed this new one as she walked into the room for group therapy. Everyone seemed to be busily evaluating each other, as they vied for the title of the "Skinniest."

Soon she would figure out new tricks to add to her repertoire. At weigh-ins, she hid a tape recorder in her underwear so she appeared heavier. She'd drink as much water as possible to add a temporary pound or two.

TALK TO CHILDREN IF THEY . . .

- Start worrying about their weight, no matter what it is.
- Start berating themselves and their bodies.
- Start changing their eating patterns, become vegetarians, refuse meals, attempt to diet, or eat secretly.
- Start wearing layers of clothes to hide thinness.
- Stop gaining weight or start losing weight with no known medical reason to account for it.

At home, she had prided herself on how long she could

go without a meal. One day. Two days. Here, she let the staff know she hated having her meals monitored, hated to be forced to eat with a group of her peers.

The school classes, nutrition education, and daily therapy made only so much difference. She kept insisting to her guilt-stricken parents that there was nothing wrong with her. She was glad when her weight dropped to seventy.

Her tombstone could read: She Died Thin.[26]

These are the worst-case scenarios, the out-of-control situations. They are real-life accounts of kids a few years older than your own. Children who are eight, nine, and ten are almost always just flirting with disaster. Those who are eleven and twelve are coming closer to serious trouble.

And that's exactly what we don't want to happen to our daughters and sons. We want to stop the problem now, before it is a life-and-death struggle. That is the point of this book.

An Ounce of Prevention

Eating disorders are easier to prevent than to cure. But when looking for early warning signs, it's hard to separate the normal ups and downs of preadolescence from the dangers of anorexia and bulimia.

Keep in mind that any dieting can be risky business for

children. They're still growing. They're more vulnerable to the effects of dehydration. The hormonal effects are more pronounced.

As soon as you see possible clues that an unsupervised diet is taking on too much importance, step in. Just don't step too hard, particularly not at first. Eating disorders become the turf on which control issues are fought between parent and child. You don't want to inadvertently set off the opening battles.

A variety of eating disorder experts, whose names and credentials are listed in the back of the book (pages 151-152), offered the following warning signs that could alert you. However, they cautioned that parents are so frequently involved with juggling life's responsibilities, so close to the problem, that signs are missed until late in the struggle. By then the children are in harm's way.

SEEK OUTPATIENT OR INPATIENT CARE IF CHILDREN . . .

- Start complaining about various physical problems: cramps, sore throats, hair loss, cold intolerance, dizziness, delay in onset of menses.
- Start thumb sucking, nail biting, head banging.
- Start exhibiting endless energy, including pacing while eating; or the reverse, extreme lethargy.
- Start denying they are hungry or lying about eating in general.
- Stop attending events at which they have to eat in front of others.

Power Struggles

Parents know that peculiar behavior among children comes and goes. Sometimes it requires parental action, if only to understand better what's going on in their lives. But many times the best thing to do is nothing. Let the behavior play itself out in the knowledge that it will flare up and then disappear.

We may walk in their bedroom and see the walls covered with photos of emaciated models. We could hear of whispered pledges among a circle of friends for a contest to determine who can lose the most weight by the end of school.

Our stomach knots in anxiety, but a few weeks later those posters have been replaced with ones of horses and the diets were forgotten by the next trip to the mall.

With other children, there are transient concerns about sudden body changes. They have a growth spurt. They start to develop sooner and more noticeably than the other students. They are self-conscious. They get alarmed, but then they move on with their lives.

Sometimes, though, these aren't phases. They may develop into serious conditions. Inevitably we, the parents, are drawn in. Dealing with an eating disorder becomes a family matter. It is a power struggle. It is a frustrating, angering, tearful battle of wills. It is the ultimate food fight. It can also be terrifying.

While we're wrestling with this problem on a day-to-day basis, the horror stories may take over our thoughts. If that happens, we should remind ourselves that most people involved with eating disorders fall into a large in-between group that seeks and finds help.

They don't snap out of it. They don't die from it. Mainly, they eventually find a way to deal with it. Sometimes it's the way we'd least expect.

chapter 15

nonfat popcorn and rice cakes

Strange Rituals and Dreaded Holidays

Looking back I realize that my daughter, Pamela, had no control in her life. We lived in three different cities in three years. On top of everything, she broke her wrist. She got depressed. She started going around with wilder kids. For the first time she failed a course.

That summer on our family vacation we took some photos. She looked at herself and said, "I'm fat." But she wasn't. Still she was seeing the world through her eyes, and that's what they told her.

My younger sister showed up for a visit and was on a diet. Pamela went on the diet with her. Together they got into a routine. They both lost weight, and people praised them. At that point it wasn't even an issue. I didn't think of dieting as similar to drinking. Most people don't get addicted. Some do.

Pamela got "addicted" to losing weight.

The first lesson I learned was there are three things a mother can't control in her children: eating, sleeping, and bowel movements. An eating disorder effects them all.

Pamela started to develop strange rituals. There were only certain foods she would eat. She'd get mad if any of us touched her special food by mistake. She would blot her food with a napkin in case there was any fat on it. She drank diet Coke, then just water. After a while it was lettuce and cantaloupes. Next she lived on nonfat popcorn and rice cakes. That was all.

She would chew slowly, endlessly.

She had a box filled with recipes for food that she never ate. She kept the refrigerator stuffed with cookie dough. She would make all this food and want everybody to eat. But not her. She read the labels of every food that came into the house. She stopped joining us at the table for meals.

Every holiday was affected. Everything we celebrate in America revolves around food. Pamela dreaded holidays. They were tearful occasions. She knew she was expected to be with other people—and to eat.

How could she do that when she kept her scale under her end table next to her bed? In the morning before she put her foot on the floor, she would pull the scale out and weigh herself. She no longer could control what she ate and what she didn't.

A Lonely Disorder

She stopped having her period. Her breath smelled sweet because the protein was breaking down the muscle. The hair on her head started to fall out. On her back and arms, though, hair started to grow. It's the body trying to keep itself warm. Her skin became dry; her eyes appeared sunken. She was exhausted a lot of the time.

About six or seven months into it, I realized I had to do something. She was isolating herself so much. She looked awful.

She ran around the house, screaming, "I'm fat. I'm so fat."

In frustration I wanted to yell back at her, "Just snap out of it. You're killing yourself. How can you do that? Where is your head? Sit down at the table and eat!"

Instead I tried to remind myself maybe it's better to say "I'm fat" rather than "I'm a terrible person."

Then she moved on to "I'm so ugly."

Food and not eating were the focus of her life. She could function at school, but not socially, and not at home.

It's such a lonely disorder. But she thought it was her friend.

She was five feet three. When her weight dropped to eighty pounds, I knew she couldn't stop. She didn't plan this in the first place, she didn't choose it, and now her eating patterns were beyond her control.

Two Carrot Strips

At first my husband, Bill, thought I was exaggerating. He didn't want to believe what was happening. He got angry. He couldn't believe his own eyes.

Finally, though, we took the parents' first steps. We set up appointments with her pediatrician, a nutritionist, and then a family therapist. The pediatrician didn't know much about eating disorders. The nutritionist had to reschedule, and the therapist said, "You know there's no cure for anorexia. Twenty percent die."

We found another therapist. This one told us never to mention the word "food" to Pamela. Never try to get her to eat. For me, doing nothing was harder than doing something. I gained thirty pounds.

Beyond the control factor, I started looking around for what might be at the heart of this problem. The therapist talked about the parents' roles. Bill wasn't around very much. His job involved a lot of travel. When he was home, Pamela might have seen him as domineering. Around him the woman's role was not so good.

Fathers seem to get fearful of their daughters when they get their period. Should they hug them the way they once did? That's hard for dads. Maybe that combined with my perception, that women are not able to do as much as men in the work world, made her decide to remain a little girl.

Pamela and I originally were close. I guess we were too close. She was trying to break away from me as an adolescent and wasn't doing well at it. I felt sorry for my dear daughter.

For my sanity, I gave the control of Pamela to Bill. I relinquished all my parental rights. He took over, and it began to work. Once I stopped trying to control her, I started to learn to just be there for her. To be supportive, but not to allow it to rule my life. I let go.

I stopped asking her to come to the table at night. I tried not to notice what she ate. Of course, inside, I still monitored what she was doing. Once we ate out and she had two carrot strips. That made my day.

I learned to pick my battles. It wasn't important what she wore to school, how many earrings she had, or whether her room was a mess. When she would talk, I'd listen, even if I didn't agree with her. There were times she would lie to me or tell me what I didn't want to hear.

I would think, "Thank God, she's talking to me."

I learned to let her make choices.

I don't think I was overly controlling when she was growing up. But when she was an eighteen-month-old baby, I could have asked, "Pamela, which book do you want me to read?" At three years old, I could have asked, "Do you want apple or grape juice?" If I'd given her choices, maybe she would have been strong enough to listen to my opinions.

One Small, Safe Food

How did it end? Each person is different.

With Pamela it came about in an unexpected way. She started going around with a nightmare of a boy. He was older, a ninth grader who had been in three drug treatment programs and partied at his home. Together they smoked grass, marijuana. It made her feel hungry. That was good, since he liked his girlfriends with a little fat on them. He didn't think she looked as good as she could.

She started to eat.

It didn't end abruptly. She didn't sit down one day and consume a burger and fries. Instead she would find one small, safe food. Then there was another safe food. It took her three months to start eating. Then it took another six months to get back to near normal.

She still watches what she eats. Putting bacon bits on a salad is a big deal. She recently ate a half a piece of pie.

When we were in the middle of this, I felt a sense of family shame and embarrassment. I didn't tell the neighbors. I didn't tell the women I play tennis with. An eating disorder makes it seem like there's something wrong with your family, that you're dysfunctional.

Now I talk to people. I feel I want to warn them. My

daughter's experience with anorexia was more fearful than anything any of my children have gone through. It can mean death.

Is she cured? I don't know. I like to think she is, and I always hope for the best.

chapter 16

anonymous overeaters

The Family Puzzle

The most likely candidates for eating disorders are often described as our best and our brightest. They are Wonder Women in waiting, with solid grades and full schedules.

They are driven kids, sweet kids, kids who want to succeed and to please. Yet their self-esteem suddenly registers zero. They have learned that at their age their skills and talents receive little peer recognition. Depressed and frustrated, they may blame parents. They declare a secret war of independence.

"How could that be?" you wonder. You blame them. You blame yourself. You blame your spouse. You blame each other. And in addition to society's heavy hand in molding our daughters, family interaction, of course, must be factored in.

(For more detailed profiles of those with eating disorders

and their parents, see chapter nine. Although the descriptions are generalities, where they ring true, they may help in putting this problem into a context.)

Some households are toxic to their members. Adults give themselves permission to abuse the children. Particularly if there is sexual abuse, an eating disorder may result. The same is true if a parent abuses alcohol or drugs. Youngsters may turn to food for similar reasons—comfort and escape.

A family history of depression or various personality disorders should also be considered. But beyond that, for the majority, while all parents play a role in shaping their children, this moment is not the time to be distracted by deciding how to measure out blame.

Later you and your kids, together and separately, can sort through and adjust the pieces of your family puzzle. You will have to alter certain behavior patterns.

But right now there is work to do. With anorexia comes the pressure to take action before the biology of starvation sets in. Once that internal mechanism occurs, it becomes extremely difficult to stop these eating habits. With bulimia there's the double fear of heart failure . . . or a possible suicide.

Because of that fear, you should make a mental inventory of what's been going on in and outside the home during the six months to a year before this eating pattern began. Have there been unsettling events, such as a grandparent's death or the breakup with a boyfriend, that could have triggered this?

Through conversations, you can try to help your children discover what the real problems are while knowing that young kids can't always easily express complex thoughts. You should try to encourage them to talk, with the focus on their lives, not food. Try to deemphasize even talking about weight. It's a trap. It opens up chances for lying.

People with eating disorders become secretive. They also have a certain sense of triumph. They feel nobody can make them do what they don't want to do. Ultimately, though, these eating patterns are dangerous conditions that can be life threatening. When they begin to take over the youngsters' lives and that of their families, then it's time for professional intervention.

Flying Blind

There is no mandatory accreditation for those who treat eating disorders. There is no universal treatment for adolescents, let alone preteens, eight to twelve. There are no systematic, controlled studies available. For the parent in search of help, it's a little like flying blind.

So, what do you do? First children should be checked by a physician to rule out any unrelated health issue. Before

DIAGNOSTIC CRITERIA

Large numbers of teens and younger children do not meet the following criteria but still have an eating disorder. Many of those individuals suffer a similar degree of psychologic distress as those who meet the strict diagnosis criteria. **Weight loss is not necessarily present in younger adolescents with the disorder.**

making that appointment, read through the following list of symptoms provided by the American Psychiatric Association. It might help you describe the child's danger signs and alert the doctor to your suspicions.

* * *

Anorexia Nervosa

A. Refusal to maintain body weight at or above a minimally normal weight for age and height (e.g., weight loss leading to maintenance of body weight less than 85 percent of that expected; or failure to make expected weight gain during period of growth, leading to body weight less than that expected).

B. Intense fear of gaining weight or becoming fat, even though underweight.

C. Disturbance in the way in which one's body weight or shape is experienced, undue influence of body weight or shape on self-evaluation, or denial of the seriousness of current low body weight.

D. In postmenarchal females, amenorrhea, i.e., the absence of at least three consecutive menstrual cycles. (A woman is considered to have amenorrhea if her periods occur only following hormones, e.g., estrogen administration.)

Restricting Type: during the current episode of Anorexia Nervosa, the person has not regularly engaged in binge-eating or purging behavior (i.e., self-induced vomiting or the misuse of laxatives, diuretics, or enemas).

Binge-Eating/Purging Type: during the current episode of Anorexia Nervosa, the person regularly engaged in binge-eating or purging behavior (i.e., self-induced vomiting or the misuse of laxatives, diuretics, or enemas).

Bulimia Nervosa

A. Recurrent episodes of binge eating. An episode of binge eating is characterized by both of the following:

(1) eating, in a discreet period of time (e.g., within any two-hour period), an amount of food that is definitely larger than most people would eat during a similar period of time under similar circumstances.

(2) a sense of lack of control over eating during the episode (e.g., a feeling that one cannot stop eating or control what or how much one is eating).

B. Recurrent inappropriate compensatory behavior in order to prevent weight gain, such as self-induced vomiting; misuse of laxatives, diuretics, enemas, or other medications; fasting; or excessive exercise.

C. The binge eating and inappropriate compensatory behaviors both occur, on average, at least twice a week for three months.

D. Self-evaluation is unduly influenced by body shape and weight.

E. The disturbance does not occur exclusively during episodes of Anorexia Nervosa.

Purging Type: during the current episode of Bulimia Nervosa, the person regularly engages in self-induced vomiting or the misuse of laxatives, diuretics, or enemas.

Nonpurging Type: during the current episode of Bulimia

Nervosa, the person has used other inappropriate compensatory behaviors, such as fasting or excessive exercise, but does not regularly engage in self-induced vomiting or the misuse of laxatives, diuretics, or enemas.

Going Public

Some medical professionals still don't expect to see anyone under the age of fifteen with an eating disorder. They don't expect to see children of color. And they don't expect to see boys.

With that caution, if anorexia or bulimia is diagnosed, you could ask for a referral or treatment suggestions.

In a nonemergency situation, you might call one or more of the organizations listed in the back of this book. They'll be able to provide you with local referrals for psychiatrists and psychologists in this area of specialty, as well as the names of various inpatient and outpatient facilities. Your immediate questions can be answered free of charge.

If your child's school has a counselor, check with that

A DAUGHTER SPEAKS— BARBIE DOLL BLUES

I look through magazines and feel I have to compete against those models. They make me want to change my body. I want to look like a Barbie doll.

But that's in my dreams. In real life I've lived every day being overweight. In third grade I went to a birthday party. There was only one other girl and the rest were boys. Most of the boys didn't even know me, but they made fun of my weight for, well, it felt like an eternity.

The pain hurt like a cut. It has scarred me for life.

My mom's always on some diet. She works out twice during the week and both days on the weekend. She tells me to come along. I'd feel stupid in front of those strangers; I don't go.

Instead, for about three months now I've been eating and then making myself throw up. I guess it's called an person. This is a prevalent problem. Once you go public even to this limited extent, you might be surprised how many others have been in the same situation. Talk to them. Regardless of the age of the people with eating disorders, if they have been involved in some type of treatment, they probably will have advice, opinions, and more referrals.

Early on you learn that there are no miracle cures. You may have to try several individual therapists, programs, or approaches before you find the right match. For example, you might find some initial success by coming at the problem somewhat indirectly and experimenting with the following kinds of possibilities.

Contact an osteopath or massage therapist. Explain what you are dealing with, power struggles manifested by eating disorders. Your children are in need of touch because they are out of touch with their bodies. You want them physically to feel peace, not pain. Can they help?

Encourage your children to attend stress reduction or

---

eating disorder. The other day when I was at cheerleading practice, I got really pale and lost my balance. I couldn't help myself. I felt dizzy and weak.

I lost some weight and gained it back. It's like riding a roller coaster. Some of the other students are beginning to notice, but I just blow it off. I thought my parents would figure it out, but they haven't. I worry, "Is this getting serious?" I tried to stop, but I feel sick after I eat. I have to throw up or I don't feel any better. I want to lose more weight.

Some kids want to be a couple of sizes smaller just because they want a certain skirt or pants. I want to be slim so people won't talk bad about me anymore. I wonder, "How will my life be when I'm skinny? Will it be different? Will it be better?" Please, it just has to.
—Millicent, age twelve

---

relaxation courses where they learn meditation, yoga, or tai chi chuan. This might allow them to replace their obsession with food and exercise with something healthy. It could also give them a sense of serenity and lower their anxiety level.

Talk to a professional in the field of acupressure or acupuncture. Ask them if they have experience using their techniques to relieve pain and increase the appetite. If the answer is yes, schedule a trial appointment or two to see how your children react to this approach.

Don't forget the power of prayer.

You've been dealing with this problem in isolation. It's time to share the emotional burden.

Catch-22

People with eating disorders don't want to be helped by others. They don't want to be anybody's patient. They want to do everything for themselves.

The Price You Pay

Before you decide which might be the best treatment, if you have insurance, check with your carrier for an explanation of the fine print of your policy. With the rise in medical costs, insurance companies are beginning to classify eating disorders as a psychiatric problem, not a medical one. Psychiatric coverage is limited in a way that medical coverage isn't.

Because of insurance restrictions, treatment options vary depending on your plan, as well as on what is available where you live. One family talks about trying to balance their love and concern for their daughter with what their plan would cover. They were frustrated that medical insurance even had to be a factor.

TYPICAL TREATMENTS

Below are listed the treatments for anorexia and bulimia suggested by the American Anorexia/Bulimia Association. In a field where the youngest victims have only recently been acknowledged, new methods and combinations of treatment are being devised. In emergency situations, you may first have to save your child's life before you can cure her.

Anorexia	Bulimia
Medical evaluation, though blood tests are often normal despite significant physical impairment	Medical evaluation, including dental examination
Individual and/or group psychotherapy to resolve conflicts, improve self-esteem	Individual and/or group psychotherapy: —cognitive, to change misconceptions —behavioral, to lessen binges —interpersonal, to improve relationships
Support groups offer important benefits when part of a comprehensive treatment plan	Support groups offer important benefits when part of a comprehensive plan
Nutritional counseling, to restore weight, provide information about healthy eating	Nutritional counseling, to avoid fasting and binges
Medication, sometimes helpful for associated physical or emotional discomforts	Medication: antidepressants have high success rate: lessening binges, improving moods, reducing weight obsession; but relapse is common unless combined with therapy
Hospitalization is sometimes needed for weight gain	Hospitalization may be needed for weight gain and to manage suicide prevention

chapter 17

taking its course

Bolts of Anger

When Andrea, my daughter, was in sixth grade, the smartest kid in class died of bulimia. It happened on the playground while he was waiting to be picked for one of the teams.

He and Andrea had grown up together, and his whole short life he'd been teased because of his weight. Fat Boy was one of the kinder names he was called.

It took his parents a long time before they could talk about the cause of his death. They couldn't make sense of why he had died of something that should have never happened in the first place. When I started to feel that something was wrong with Andrea, I was immediately concerned.

Then my husband found evidence: a bag. Our daughter had thrown up into a brown paper bag and left it hidden, but not hidden very well. I knew she had been losing weight.

Now my worry increased. I asked her directly, "Is something wrong?" She stopped talking and left the room.

I tried to analyze what was happening. Emotionally I had seen a change. Her even keel, her good temperament were gone, replaced by lightning bolts of anger. Was it adolescence . . . or something more?

Just in case, I brought home information about eating disorders. "It can affect your heart, your teeth, your skin," I said. Scare tactics didn't work. I backed off.

I started thinking about our family. We have three children. Andrea's the one with the most gifts, in sports, in intelligence, in performance in school. Who would have ever thought her weakness would be emotional security?

As time passed I started pushing for help. "No," she'd say. "I can handle it." But she couldn't. I felt caught in the dilemma of how long was too long to let her assert control before there was a real risk of medical fallout.

Instead the fallout came from another source. She got picked up for stealing junk food—snacks—from the supermarket. I felt I had no choice but to lay down my own law. "You have to see a doctor," I said. I wanted to start with an M.D. for a physical, then a psychiatrist.

My husband and I have separate insurance plans. With HMOs the attitude is, "Oh, bulimia can be cured in eight therapy sessions."

When I called, I said, "I've heard some plans cover up to a month of hospitalization."

"Not yours," was the answer.

The other plan gave me the name of a single participating center in our area that provided group therapy. Andrea didn't want to go there. She wanted to go to a doctor outside the plan. When we agreed, this man saw her for a few minutes and told her, "It's not life threatening." As long as she didn't carry it to an extreme, she didn't need any further medical tests, and certainly not hospitalization.

She was five feet four and about 102 pounds. Her weight wasn't life threatening, but the behavior pattern was. I felt he was giving her permission to continue.

A Dare

Andrea told me she got the idea from a TV program. I suspect she and her girlfriends came up with a dare, a group experiment. They have the same coach. They were really into volleyball. She played so hard, she'd tear the ligaments in her legs.

Then she and her friends all got into body beautiful. Andrea's impressionable, the kind to follow others into a trap. She wasn't the only one among them with an eating disorder.

She brought home the names of therapists. "The one you want to see doesn't even have enough credits to do counseling in a high school." I said. I thought she should see someone who'd graduated from a reputable school, trained in this specialty, and passed various licensing tests.

That stuff didn't matter to her.

We got into heated discussions, or there was silence. I studied her body language. I tried to look her in the eyes. She ducked her head. She didn't want me to peer into her soul. I wondered, "What evil does she think she has done?" In my heart I knew she had done nothing.

Losers on Prozac

I read more about bulimia, the possible relationship to a family history of depression, alcoholism, and so on. Among our relatives there had been a suicide attempt and an alcohol problem.

Andrea went to Overeaters Anonymous. She went to a therapist, then a psychiatrist. She wanted to go alone, not with her father or me. This doctor prescribed Prozac for her and I think it helped, but she hated it.

She rebelled at the idea of being diagnosed with a mental disorder or taking medication. "Only losers take Prozac," she said, and quit taking it.

The bulimia flared up again. I called the doctor and suggested family therapy. He refused. He didn't "want to undermine her trust" in him. He asked me about her eating patterns.

"It's a very private thing," I told him. "In the family, she doesn't even discuss this with her sisters. God only knows what goes through her mind when she eats."

He asked about the family. I told him my husband was easygoing. He had his standards, then he put his foot down. But mainly he let Andrea do her thing. He realized she might be depressed. He felt she would get better.

I told him that I couldn't say we'd ever had any kind of family crisis. Our kids have had uneventful lives. I was never heavy into discipline. We never fretted over Andrea. We let her do what she wanted. I tried to lay a good basic foundation. I took them to church, trained them in the right way of doing things, and let go.

And then our insurance companies announced she had hit the wall. They would no longer cover her treatment.

Small Steps of Suicide

Sometimes I wish I could verbally shake her out of it. But the doctors and therapists seem to say there are worse ways for depression to manifest itself. And, by the way, not all bulimics—even those for whom Prozac is successful—suffer from depression.

I know I can't further control the situation. That would be detrimental. It's in Andrea's hands. I see that self-destruction is part of it. I see the cycle now. When she starts getting upset, she goes into it. Then she calms down and comes out of it. Still I fear, is it small steps toward suicide?

Part of me just waits in the wings praying that my daughter will find the answer herself. The other part keeps silently looking, talking, and researching the subject. I need something more than letting the bulimia take its course.

chapter 18

road to recovery

Painful and Confusing

Children with eating disorders have been coping with life by focusing on food. Therapy can help give them different coping weapons as their symptoms diminish.

This is a painful and confusing time for parents and your offspring. Anorexics and bulimics have to deal with the idea of getting better—and bigger. Simultaneously, they're afraid to let go of a structure they have been using for a comparatively long time.

All the problems that were being ignored now come to the surface.

Previously thoughtful, considerate behavior gives way to hostile, demanding, petulant attitudes. And there you are. You are bright and successful. You know how to negotiate your own world, but now you may feel you can't help your own kid. You may feel like a failure.

But let's say the weight loss continues. Hospitalization should be considered. Again, consult with the therapist, a doctor—and your insurance carrier to see what they cover. Some hospitals provide both outpatient and inpatient care, and the care is a team effort. Patients have the advantage of medical, psychiatric, and nutritional counseling all in one place. Plus, the various aspects of the treatment program are coordinated.

In some situations, a "contract" with goals is negotiated between the patients and staff. A system of rewards is based on meeting the goals and gaining weight. The staff works together to teach patients how to eat, how to trust, and how to deal with life by getting together and talking.

There is individual therapy, group therapy, and, especially for young children, family therapy. Patients and their parents—and sometimes their siblings—discuss many issues. Parents are encouraged to talk openly about recovery. You discuss your fears that your daughters may be hospitalized again.

You're also encouraged to verbalize your feelings of guilt for putting your children in a hospital while they are protesting and believing that there is nothing wrong.

It can be cathartic for parents. Perhaps for the first time in a long time you can look at your children and see them once again as individuals instead of as a problem. They are people with an illness, but first they are people. They are unique, as you are.

Fifteen Thousand Hours of TV

Parents are in a bind. By the time kids reach first grade, they have already processed enough information at home, from TV, and from the world around them to have developed prejudices about what is the perfect body size: slim with sleek muscles. In school, they know that when it comes to popularity, thin gets the prize; chubby gets the teasing.

A SON'S LAMENT

I'm a little pudgy. I used to weigh 140 pounds, but now I weigh 121, almost twenty pounds lighter! My dad hasn't even noticed. He still picks on me and calls me Tub. I ignore him, but in my mind I'd like to beat him up or make fun of him like he does to me. My mom is heavy, too, and Dad thinks it's okay to talk about the size of her stomach.

—**Jason, age thirteen**

As the years go by, you cannot monitor your children's every waking moment. You can worry, though, that by the time they finish high school most of them will have spent eleven thousand hours in school and fifteen thousand hours watching TV.[28]

They sit there, transfixed, soaking up the messages: Be sexy, be cool, be sophisticated, and be lean. They sit there, transfixed, filling their mouths with whatever food is available.

What can you do to change this picture?

You can pay attention to both your children's sense of self and their food intake. It would be great if there were ten easy steps to keep your kids—and their stomachs—well fed with love and a balanced diet. Instead, it's more about instinct. It also involves trying to tune in a little more to the subtleties going on in your children's lives.

Here's a place to start. To help protect them from being overwhelmed by the messages they sponge up from the culture, you can talk to your kids about the reality behind these pictures. You can encourage them to continue to explore within the framework of seeing the world realistically, being tough, and learning how to be self-protective.

You can remind yourself that they may want some freedom, they may be separating from you, but they don't want you to abandon them. And, finally, you can work to change society into a less violent and more nurturing place.

That's not just a pipe dream. It just has to be broken down into digestible pieces. On the home front, for instance, let's say you hear your youngsters floating trial balloons of negative comments about themselves. Almost as throwaway lines, they say that they feel fat and ugly. They feel left out. They feel bad for whatever reason.

You know that really they're searching for comfort and verbal hugs. It's often hard to stop what you're doing, listen, and give them specific positive feedback. But that extra effort right now can make a crucial difference later.

In other words, don't just say, "You look fine," and then go back to the division report that's due the next morning. They need more. You can take a few minutes, put everything aside, and talk with them. Fish around. Try to find out what led them to make that kind of statement.

Then not only tell them what wonderful people they are but also remind them about their attributes. Be honest and realistic. Talk about *their* strengths, *your* strengths, how they bring great joy in your life. Keep shifting the conversation back to what makes them special: their spelling ability, talent as a mimic, warmth toward others.

They should be given increased responsibility at home and then complimented for the proficient way they do those tasks. You want to make them see and appreciate their inner beauty, their willingness to be adventurous, and their continuing strength.

And now, here are a few quick do's and don'ts about their stomachs.

Role Models

You're treading a difficult path. If your youngsters' food-diet-weight decision is heading toward an eating disorder, you don't want to encourage it. But, still, if their appraisal of themselves as overweight is realistic, you don't want to deny this. You owe them your honesty.

Adults have to be careful when they start suggesting children lose weight. Any parents who think their kids don't know they have a weight problem are wrong.

Instead, parents should look for positive role models, public figures, and family friends who have the same physical characteristics as your child. Children need to see real-life examples that show that physical differences don't automatically mean they'll miss out on success and happiness.

STOMACH POWER

Do give your kids a personal food and snack shelf stocked with healthy options in premeasured portions.

Don't freak if they suddenly decide to live exclusively on Chicken McNuggets. Most likely it's temporary.

Don't completely deny your children junk food. They'll sneak off to a friend's house to have it or will buy it on their own.

Don't talk about starving children wherever. You're setting up a future power struggle and taking away the kids' ability to decide whether they are hungry or full.

Do allow your children as much choice and control as possible over what they eat.

Don't try to resolve conflict through food. Conflicts should be talked about.

Get out the family album and show them pictures of you at their age. There's a good chance you looked a lot like they do now. Maybe your nickname was Biscuits because you ate too many of those little white rolls. Tell them what you went through, how you felt about your size, and how you survived similar situations.

They may not realize that you went through any equally painful and silly moments. In their concerns about their bodies, they may think they are the only ones to have these troubling feelings. They may forget that others are teased and even ridiculed for their shape.

Never forget that you are your kids' first and most important role model. You have to teach them healthy ways to solve problems. If you avoid them, so will your children. As parents, you should say, "It's okay to talk about problems." This simple statement, of course, could involve a whole change in the mindset and patterns of behavior of your family. It may mean you have to turn to family therapy in order to learn how to face difficulties directly and discuss them in the process.

This type of radical change involves an enormous

SOUND FAMILIAR?

I'm very close to my aunt, and she would come to my house often. She'd stay all day and eat nothing but a piece of cheese. She saw herself as fat, when in reality she was skinny.

My family worried because she got sickly looking, as if she was torturing herself. We think what finally made her stop was she got pregnant. Now she looks back at pictures of herself during this period and comments on how she looked.

She vows never to do it again, and she encourages me and my family to be proud of our bodies and never do anything to harm them. But you know what? The food fight in her head isn't over. It still goes on. It's just quieter now.

—Becky, age thirteen

amount of work. But before dismissing it entirely, remember that kids who grow up in families where problems aren't faced are more at risk in general, and more at risk specifically to develop eating disorders. And unless these habits are broken and new ones put into place, it will remain difficult for your children to change their response to the problem.

You should think about your own behavior. What are you communicating to your children about growing up? About sexuality? About their bodies? About their gender? Maybe you feel uncomfortable with the idea that they are getting older. You worry about their physical and emotional safety.

It's more than many parents want to handle. You may have always felt that your own body didn't measure up to what you'd like. You may be conveying entire volumes of unspoken messages to your kids about your own sense of insecurity about how you look.

What are your feelings about your own body, food, exercise, dieting, your preoccupation with weighing yourself all the time? Think about whether your daughters listen to your adult discussions about passing up dessert because of a fear of fat. Do you prepare meals for the family and then just nibble around the edges?

What is the interaction between you and your spouse? Do you criticize each other's looks? Do you take shots at each other about overgrown bellies and expanding backsides? Are there diet pills in your bathroom medicine cabinet?

It's not unusual for children with eating disorders to come from homes where either a parent or a close relative has also been anorexic or bulimic. They watch you. They see what you're doing. They see how you eat and what you eat. They note your exercise routines. They monitor your own worries about weight. They know if you're on an endless diet. They know if you take laxatives or diuretics. They may even sneak them from your medicine cabinet. They emulate your behavior.

You are responsible for the messages you give your kids.

They may not listen to you when you're trying to get them to clean up their bedrooms, set the table, or watch their little brother. But their hearing shuts down even further if you send the very mixed message about why they should have a healthy diet while you're downing a slice or two of pepperoni pizza.

Show them, instead, through your own daily eating habits.

The Shape of Love

Confronting an eating disorder can be a terrible time for a family. But most kids get through it. In the end is the beginning. Many youngsters who have dealt with this issue go into adolescence with much clearer thinking.

You can get through it, too. You just shouldn't forget to love your children. Remember some of the things that have

SOUND FAMILIAR?

Ever since I can remember, my mom has cared about what she eats. She was thin, and to make sure she stayed that way, she did aerobics every morning. Then with her job, she couldn't keep up with her exercising. She gained weight.

She started to go on numerous diets, none of which worked. She went back to her morning stretches and exercises, but she still wasn't happy with herself. When she stepped on the scale, she was upset. She waited a week to weigh herself again.

She had gained two more pounds. She freaked. I tried to tell her she lost fat and gained muscle. I said, "It doesn't matter how much you weigh. It's how you look and feel about yourself."

She gave me one of those mother looks and said, "Well, I'm sorry, but I won't feel good until I reach the weight that I'm comfortable with."

—Zoe, age twelve

been said. Kids are people, with their own feelings, thoughts, and opinions. Listen to them.

You may not agree with or like those opinions, but try to avoid power struggles. Praise your children as much as possible. Tell them you value them. Help them develop a good sense of self-esteem. Work on communication skills. Refrain from too much criticism. Focus on the positive, and get professional help if you feel it's needed.

And, finally, tell and show your kids that you love and accept them at any weight.

PART III

For All Readers

chapter 19

help
yourself

Help Is a Phone Call Away

Below is a list of organizations involved with the issues of eating disorders, healthy eating, and children's well-being. The types of help that these groups can supply range from the name of a local pediatrician to written material for a school paper on those topics.

ACADEMY FOR EATING DISORDERS
Montefiore Medical School—Adolescent Medicine
111 E. 210th Street
Bronx, NY 10467
(718) 920-6782

Provides advocates for the field, promotes effective treatment, stimulates research, sponsors international conferences, develops prevention initiatives.

AMERICAN ACADEMY OF PEDIATRICS (AAP)
P.O. Box 927
Elk Grove Village, IL 60007-0927
(708) 228-5005
E-mail: kidsdocs@aap.org

Provides pediatric referrals to specific geographic locations, as well as a brochure on eating disorders.

AMERICAN ANOREXIA/BULIMIA ASSOCIATION (AABA)
293 Central Park West, Suite #1-R
New York, NY 10024
(212) 501-8351
(212) 501-0342 (fax)

Provides written information and nationwide referrals for therapists, professional training, treatment centers, and support groups.

AMERICAN EATING DISORDER CENTER
330 W. 58th Street
New York, NY 10019
(212) 582-5190

Provides outpatient clinical services, referrals, and educational materials.

ANOREXIA NERVOSA & RELATED EATING DISORDERS, INC. (ANRED)
P.O. Box 5102
Eugene, OR 97405
(541) 344-1144

Collects and distributes information about eating and exercise disorders through booklets and a monthly newsletter, and provides training, workshops, and speakers on the issue.

CENTER FOR SCIENCE IN THE PUBLIC INTEREST (CSPI)
KIDS AGAINST JUNK FOOD (KAJF)
1875 Connecticut Avenue, NW
Washington, DC 20009-5728
(202) 332-9110

CSPI leads a nationwide campaign to improve America's diet and health, including pressuring fast-food restaurants and schools to improve their menus.

KAJF helps elementary and high school kids to eat healthy diets through action programs.

CENTER FOR THE STUDY OF ANOREXIA AND BULIMIA
1 W. 91st Street
New York, NY 10024
(212) 595-3449

Providesoutreach, outpatient treatment, and therapist training.

CHILDREN'S BETTER HEALTH INSTITUTE
P.O. Box 567
1100 Waterway Blvd.
Indianapolis, IN 46206
(317) 636-8881

Publishes magazines for eight- to twelve-year-olds about health, fitness, and nutrition.

EATING DISORDERS AWARENESS AND PREVENTION (EDAP)
603 Stewart Street #803
Seattle, WA 98101
(206) 386-3587

Sponsors Eating Disorders Awareness Week each February with a network of state coordinators, educational material, and programs.

THE EATING DISORDERS CENTER/SCHNEIDER CHILDREN'S HOSPITAL OF LONG ISLAND JEWISH MEDICAL CENTER
269-01 76th Avenue
New Hyde Park, NY 11040
(718) 470-3270
(718) 347-2315 (fax)

Provides a multidisciplinary approach to the treatment of children and adolescents with eating disorders, including assessment, psychotherapies, and nutritional counseling on an outpatient and inpatient basis.

(Around the nation there are similar facilities with multidisciplinary treatment programs. Some are in public hospital locations; others are private. Accreditation and insurance acceptation varies.)

INFORMATION RESOURCES AND INQUIRIES BRANCH NATIONAL INSTITUTE OF MENTAL HEALTH
5600 Fishers Lane #15C-05
Rockville, MD 20857

Provides information about mental disorders.

INTERNATIONAL ASSOCIATION OF EATING DISORDERS PROFESSIONALS (IAEDP)
123 NW 13th Street #206
Boca Raton, FL 33432
(800) 800-8126
(407) 338-9913 (fax)

Provides certification, education, workshops, and an annual symposium. A membership organization for professionals.

NATIONAL ASSOCIATION OF ANOREXIA NERVOSA & ASSOCIATED DISORDERS (ANAD)
P.O. Box 7
Highland Park, IL 60035
(847) 831-3438
(847) 433-4632 (fax)

Holds national conferences; sponsors support groups, research, and a crisis hotline; provides free materials and speakers to educate students.

NATIONAL ASSOCIATION TO ADVANCE FAT ACCEPTANCE, INC. (NAAFA)
P.O. Box 188620
Sacramento, CA 95818
(800) 442-1214

Works to end discrimination and empower fat people through education, advocacy, and member support.

NATIONAL EATING DISORDERS ORGANIZATION (NEDO)
affiliated with Laureate
Eating Disorders Program
6655 S. Yale Avenue
Tulsa, OK 74136
(918) 481-4044

Focuses on prevention, education, research, and treatment referrals.

OVEREATERS ANONYMOUS HEADQUARTERS
P.O. Box 44020
Rio Rancho, NM 87174
(505) 891-2664

Provides a twelve-step self-help fellowship. For local listings, check the telephone white pages under Overeaters Anonymous.

SHAPEDOWN
11 Library Place
San Anselmo, CA 94960
(415) 453-8886
(415) 453-8888 (fax)
E-mail: shapedown@aol.com

Provides referrals for child and adolescent obesity programs in a thousand cities nationwide, and publishes and distributes a pediatric behavior modification obesity program.

UNITED STATES DEPARTMENT OF AGRICULTURE, FOOD AND CONSUMER SERVICE
3101 Park Center Drive, #802
Alexandria, VA 22302
(703) 305-2039
(703) 304-2312 (fax)
E-mail: teamnutrition@reeusda.gov

Provides information on school breakfast and lunch programs, as well as Team Nutrition, a network of public-private partnerships that focus on nutrition and healthy children.

More Reading

American Psychiatric Association. *Diagnostic and Statistical Manual of Mental Disorders,* 4th edition. Washington, DC: American Psychiatric Association, 1994.

Aronson, Joyce Kraus. *Insights in the Dynamic Psychotherapy of Anorexia and Bulimia.* Northvale, NJ: Jason Aronson, 1993.

Bruch, Hilde. *The Golden Cage: The Enigma of Anorexia Nervosa.* Cambridge: Harvard University Press, 1978.

Chernin, Kim. *The Hungry Self: Women, Eating and Identity.* New York: Times Books, 1985.

Czyzewski, Danita, and Melanie A. Suhr, eds. *Hilde Bruch: Conversations with Anorexics.* New York: Basic Books, 1988.

Hall, Lindsey, and Leigh Cohn. *Bulimia: A Guide to Recovery.* Santa Barbara, CA: Gurze Books, 1986.

Havel, Richard J., Doris H. Calloway, Joan D. Gussow, Walter Mertz, and Malden C. Neshem. Subcommittee on the Tenth Edition of RDAs Food and Nutrition Board, Commission on Life Sciences, National Research Council. *Recommended Dietary Allowances,* 10th edition. Washington, DC: National Academy Press, 1989.

Hirschmann, Jane, and Carol Munter. *Overcoming Overeating: Living Free in a World of Food.* Reading, MA: Addison-Wesley, 1988.

———. *When Women Stop Hating Their Bodies: Freeing Yourself from Food and Weight Obsession.* New York: Fawcett Columbine, 1995.

Hirschmann, Jane, and Lela Zaphiropolous. *Solving Your Child's Eating Problems: A Completely New Approach to Raising Children Free of Food and Weight Problems.* New York: Fawcett Columbine, 1990.

Hutchinson, Marcia Germaine. *Transforming Body Image: Learning to Love the Body You Have.* Trumansburg, NY: Crossing Press, 1985.

Jacobson, Michael F., and Bruce Maxwell. *What Are We Feeding Our Kids?* New York: Workman, 1994.

Jonas, Jeffrey. *All You Need to Know about Prozac.* New York: Bantam, 1990.

Kano, Susan. *Making Peace with Food: Freeing Yourself from the Diet-Weight Obsession.* New York: Harper & Row, 1989.

Kubersky, Rachel. *Everything You Need to Know about Eating Disorders.* New York: Rosen, 1992.

Maine, Margo. *Father Hunger: Fathers, Daughters and Food.* Carlsbad, CA: Gurze Books, 1991.

Maloney, Michael, and Rachel Kranz. *Straight Talk about Eating Disorders.* New York: Facts on File, 1991.

Marx, Russell. *It's Not Your Fault: Overcoming Anorexia and Bulimia through Biopsychiatry.* New York: Villard Books, 1991.

McKay, Matthew, and Patrick Fanning, with Kirk Johnson, ed. *Self-Esteem.* Oakland, CA: New Harbinger, 1987.

Orenstein, Peggy. *Schoolgirls: Young Women, Self-Esteem, and the Confidence Gap.* New York: Doubleday, 1994.

Pipher, Mary. *Reviving Ophelia: Saving the Selves of Adolescent Girls.* New York: G. P. Putnam's Sons, 1994.

Salter, Charles A. *Looking Good, Eating Right: A Sensible Guide to Proper Nutrition and Weight Loss for Teens.* Brookfield, CT: Millbrook, 1991.

Sandbek, Terence. *The Deadly Diet: Recovering from Anorexia and Bulimia.* Oakland, CA: New Harbinger, 1986.

Scott, Derek, ed. *Anorexia and Bulimia Nervosa: Practical Approaches.* New York: New York University Press, 1988.

Siegel, Michelle, Judith Brisman, and Margot Weinshel. *Surviving an Eating Disorder: New Perspectives and Strategies for Family and Friends*. New York: Harper & Row, 1988.

Wilson, C. Philip, with Charles C. Hogan and Ira L. Mintz, eds. *Fear of Being Fat: The Treatment of Anorexia Nervosa and Bulimia*. New York: Jason Aronson, 1985.

Wolf, Naomi. *The Beauty Myth: How Images of Beauty Are Used Against Women*. New York: William Morrow, 1991.

chapter 20

my journey

The Journey and the Destination

When I start to write a book, I feel as if I'm setting out on a journey. I'm never sure what I will have learned when I reach my final destination. Before I take that first step, I create sort of a map, an outline of where I think my adventure might lead me. Then I look for help to fill in the blanks.

To gather information for this project, I turned to a range of people and books. Each time you see the word "expert," that's what I'm talking about. Because this book is for preteens and parents, I alternated between interviewing girls and boys and adults.

I typed on my computer conversations with individual students in the third through eighth grade who I met in person, on-line, or over the phone. I talked with groups of students in sixth, seventh, and eighth grade so I could learn about this issue.

Of all these people, students from two groups in particular

became my top research assistants. What I learned from them I passed on to you.

Arlene Weber Morales, Media Specialist at Marine Park School, IS 278, in Brooklyn, New York, came up with the idea that the sixth- and seventh-grade students in Janice Geary's language arts class might be interested in helping me. For a school year they exchanged ideas with me on this topic on-line by E-mail and also by snail-mail.

First they would discuss their thoughts in class, then report what conclusions they had come to. In addition, they answered my questions and sent me regular messages about their lives, their diets, and their futures. They voted on their favorite titles and chapter headings, too.

Assignments

1. Write a paragraph or two on this question:
   If you could change one thing about what you look like, what would it be?
2. Write a true story about how an eating disorder touched your life in a personal way.
   (Your brother, mom, cousin, friend, you . . .)
3. Interview a doctor, cafeteria worker, coach, nutrition expert, eating disorder expert, model, Ricki Lake, therapist/counselor on this topic. Take notes.
4. Keep a food log.
   (For one week write down what you eat and drink each day.)
5. Complete the thirteen-question

The other group was larger—several hundred. Donna Chumas, Director of Libraries, Patchogue-Medford Schools, New York, set these wheels in motion. She arranged for me to meet twice with all the eighth graders in three middle schools in the district. The first time we discussed the goals of this project, and I gave them this choice of assignments.

The next time we met, they turned in their completed

work and told me what they'd discovered. All the students were helpful, but those from Ms. Edyie Geller's classes, South Ocean Middle School, Patchogue, took the greatest care. They even suggested most of the different chapter headings for the book.

Eating Attitude Quiz.

6. Learn what you can in cyberspace. Keep a record of where you find the information.
   (Discussion groups, news groups, names of organizations, whatever)
7. Use the school computer and/or card catalog to learn what you can. Keep a record of where you find what.
   (Books, info in encyclopedia, articles)
8. Find a minimum of five famous people with an eating disorder. Keep a record of where you find the information.
9. Five title suggestions.
   (Not Pigging Out, Fed Up, and Barfing.)
10. Do nothing. This is voluntary.

Adults

Eating disorders are a global problem among the more affluent nations. I spoke with experts in New Zealand, Israel, and England. They all agreed that there has been an increase in the number of cases they see. As a Tel Aviv doctor said, "Sadly, it is a growth industry."

Here are the names and professional backgrounds of the adults I interviewed for this book. (Not listed are the names of the parents who shared information about their personal involvement with this issue. They want to protect their daughters' privacy.)

Joyce Kraus Aronson, Ph.D., editor of *Insights in the Dynamic Psychotherapy of Anorexia and Bulimia: An Introduction to the Literature;* a psychotherapist in private practice in New York City.
Lori Borrud, Dr.P.H., R.D., nutritionist, U.S. Department of Agriculture, Agricultural Research Service, "What We Eat in America" study, Washington, D.C. (Riverdale, Maryland).

Timothy D. Brewerton, M.D., director, Eating Disorders Center, Institute of Psychiatry, Medical University of South Carolina, associate professor of psychiatry and behavioral sciences.

Janet David, Ph.D., board of directors, Center for the Study of Anorexia and Bulimia; psychologist in private practice specializing in eating disorders; and a staff member of the Renfrew Center, New York City.

Gladys Foxe, C.S.W., psychotherapist in private practice specializing in nutritional counseling and eating disorders, New York City.

Bridget Forshew Funk, R.N., psychiatric nurse; health educator specializing in the inpatient treatment of adolescents, including eating disorder care, in Cincinnati, Ohio.

Neville H. Golden, M.D., codirector, Eating Disorders Center, The Schneider Children's Hospital of Long Island Jewish Medical Center, New Hyde Park, New York; author of numerous articles for professional journals.

Robert Huffer, Ph.D., family systems therapist specializing in bulimia, in Monterey, California.

Michael Jacobson, Ph.D., cofounder/executive director, Center for Science in the Public Interest, Washington, D.C.; coauthor of numerous books, including the *Fast-Food Guide* and *What Are We Feeding Our Kids?*

Betsy Gingel James, health and nutrition teacher, Rennaissance Coordinator, Laurel High School, Laurel, Maryland.

Vivian Meehan, R.N., founder/president, National Association of Anorexia Nervosa and Associated Disorders, (ANAD), Highland Park, Illinois.

Ira Mintz, M.D., psychoanalyst specializing in psychosomatic diseases; author/coeditor of numerous articles and books, including *Fear of Being Fat: The Treatment of Anorexia Nervosa and Bulimia*, Englewood, New Jersey.

Alanna Moshfegh, M.S., R.D., nutritionist, research leader, U.S. Department of Agriculture, Agricultural Research Service, "What We Eat in America" study, Washington, D.C. (Riverdale, Maryland).

Virginia Reath, M.P.H., physician's associate, gynecology, with a special interest in adolescent issues, New York City.

Jean Rubel, Th.D., founder/president, Anorexia Nervosa and Related Eating Disorders, Inc. (ANRED), Eugene, Oregon.

ENDNOTES

1. Richard J. Havel et al., *Recommended Dietary Allowances,* 10th edition (Washington, D.C.: National Academy Press, 1989).
2. Personal interview with Neville Golden, M.D.
3. Ten percent figure, American Anorexia/Bulimia Association, Inc.; twenty percent figure, Anorexia Nervosa and Related Eating Disorders, Inc.
4. Joyce Kraus Aronson, ed., *Insights in the Dynamic Psychotherapy of Anorexia and Bulimia: An Introduction to the Literature* (Northvale, NJ: Jason Aronson, 1993).
5. American Anorexia/Bulimia Association, Inc.
6. Michael Maloney and Rachel Kranz, *Straight Talk about Eating Disorders* (New York: Facts on File, 1991); personal interview with Timothy Brewerton, M.D.
7. Ten percent figure, Maloney and Kranz, *Straight Talk about Eating Disorders;* forty percent figure, American Anorexia/Bulimia Association, Inc.
8. National Institute of Mental Health.
9. Personal interview with Jean Rubel, Th.D.
10. 1940 date, personal interview with Timothy Brewerton, M.D.; 1979–80 date, Aronson, *Insights in the Dynamic Psychotherapy of Anorexia and Bulimia.*
11. Personal interview with Jean Rubel, Th.D.
12. Maryann Hammers, "Kids and Their Bodies," *New York Newsday,* February 4, 1995.
13. Brown University, *Child & Adolescent Behavior Newsletter.*
14. American Anorexia/Bulimia Association, Inc.
15. Maloney and Kranz, *Straight Talk about Eating Disorders.*
16. Personal interview with Robert Huffer, Ph.D.
17. Personal interview with Neville Golden, M.D.
18. Aronson, ed., *Insights in the Dynamic Psychotherapy of Anorexia and Bulimia.*
19. Jane Brody, "Help for Youth Beset by Eating Disorders," *New York Times,* January 31, 1996.
20. Personal interview with Neville Golden, M.D; Maloney and Kranz, *Straight Talk about Eating Disorders.*
21. The Kids' Eating Disorder Survey (KEDS): A Study of Middle School Students, Ann C. Childress, M.D.; Timothy D. Brewerton, M.D.; Elizabeth L. Hodges, M.S.W.; Mark P. Jarrell, Ph.D.; personal interview with Timothy Brewerton, M.D.
22. Jane Brody, "Rise in Obesity Explored by Experts," *New York Times,* December 6, 1994.

23. Food Marketing Industry, *1988 Yearbook on Agriculture,* U.S. Department of Agriculture.
24. Lena Williams, "What's for Lunch?" *New York Times,* October 26, 1994.
25. Personal interviews with Lori Borrud, Dr.P.H.; Michael Jacobson, Ph.D.; Elizabeth Gingel James; Alanna Moshfegh, M.S., R.D.
26. Personal interviews with Ira Mintz, M.D.; Neville Golden, M.D.; Bridget Funk.
27. John Darnton, "'Skeletal' Models Create Furor over British *Vogue,*" *New York Times,* June 3, 1996.
28. Brown University, *Child & Adolescent Behavior Newsletter.*

WITH THANKS

While researching and writing this book, I also tangled with cancer. I couldn't have maintained as normal a schedule as I did without the love and support of my family and friends. I owe them all . . . starting with my special partner, Stan Mack; my sisters, Barbara and Carolyn; my extended family, Frieda Lutze, Ernie Lutze, Pearl Mack, Kenny Mack, Peter Mack, Stephanie Ripple; and my family of friends, Linda Broessel, Phyllis Cadle, Lucy Cefalu, Donna Forsman, Jane Goldberg, Harriet and Ted Gottfried, Kay Franey, Carole Mayedo, Rosemarie and Marvin Mazor, Judy Pollock, Howie Rosen, Michael Sexton, Valerie Stern, Deborah Udin, and the members of the Third Thursday Group.